Carol Lefevre holds a PhD in Creative Writing from the University of Adelaide, where she is a Visiting Research Fellow. Her first novel *Nights in the Asylum* was shortlisted for the Commonwealth Writers' Prize and won the Nita B. Kibble Award. As well as her non-fiction book *Quiet City: Walking in West Terrace Cemetery*, Carol has published short fiction, journalism, and personal essays. She was the recipient of the 2016 Barbara Hanrahan Fellowship, and is an affiliate member of the J.M. Coetzee Centre for Creative Practice, where she was Writer-in-Residence in 2017. Her most recent book, *Murmurations*, was shortlisted for the 2021 Cristina Stead Prize for Fiction in the NSW Premier's Literary Awards, and for the Fiction Prize in the South Australian Festival Awards. Carol lives in Adelaide.

Also by Carol Lefevre

*Murmurations* (2020)
*The Happiness Glass* (2018)
*Quiet City: Walking in West Terrace Cemetery* (2016)
*If You Were Mine* (2008)
*Nights in the Asylum* (2007)

# THE TOWER

CAROL LEFEVRE

We respectfully acknowledge the wisdom of Aboriginal and Torres Strait Islander peoples and their custodianship of the lands and waterways. Spinifex offices are located on Djiru, Bunurong, Wadawurrung, Eora, and Noongar Country.

First published by Spinifex Press, 2022. Reprinted 2023

Spinifex Press Pty Ltd
PO Box 5270, North Geelong, VIC 3215, Australia
PO Box 105, Mission Beach, QLD 4852, Australia
women@spinifexpress.com.au
www.spinifexpress.com.au

Copyright © Carol Lefevre, 2022

The moral right of the author has been asserted.

All rights reserved. Without limiting the rights under copyright reserved above, no part of this publication may be reproduced, stored in or introduced into a retrieval system, or transmitted, in any form or by any means (electronic, mechanical, photocopying, recording or otherwise) without prior written permission of both the copyright owner and the above publisher of the book.

**Copying for educational purposes**
Information in this book may be reproduced in whole or part for study or training purposes, subject to acknowledgement of the source and providing no commercial usage or sale of material occurs. Where copies of part or whole of the book are made under part VB of the Copyright Act, the law requires that prescribed procedures be followed. For information contact the Copyright Agency Limited.

The quote from Margaret Olley is reproduced with permission from Meg Stewart, and the Trustees of the Margaret Olley Estate.

Edited by Pauline Hopkins and Susan Hawthorne
Cover design by Deb Snibson, MAPG
Typesetting by Helen Christie, Blue Wren Books
Typeset in Adobe Garamond
Printed by McPherson's Printing Group

 A catalogue record for this book is available from the National Library of Australia

ISBN: 9781925950625 (paperback)
ISBN: 9781925950632 (ebook)

We are all prisoners of our upbringing. Some people thrash around in that cage all their lives; only when you find the door and get out do you learn to fly.

Margaret Olley
*Margaret Olley, Far From a Still Life,* Meg Stewart

>

# CONTENTS

| | |
|---|---|
| The Tower | 1 |
| Fish | 7 |
| The Tower | 23 |
| Kandahar | 31 |
| The Tower | 51 |
| At Swan's Hotel | 61 |
| The Tower | 71 |
| Life Support | 81 |
| The Tower | 95 |
| Esperine | 101 |
| The Tower | 125 |
| The Little Flower | 133 |
| The Tower | 147 |
| Monkey Puzzle | 151 |
| The Tower | 163 |
| Dream Street | 169 |
| The Tower | 183 |
| Plunges | 189 |
| The Tower | 201 |
| Yes, No, Maybe So | 207 |
| The Tower | 221 |
| The House of First Happiness | 227 |
| The Tower | 245 |

# THE TOWER

Dorelia was driving her friend Bunty to Bowen therapy when they took a wrong turn, and then another, until at the end of a quiet cul-de-sac, set among sheltering trees, stood the most adorable house. Its front door was shadowed by a graceful porch and above the porch rose a small tower.

"Oh look!" Dorelia stopped the car.

The house was painted a pale vanilla with carriage-green trim. Above the porch was a plaster head wreathed with plaster flowers, its feminine face calm, its hooded eyes lowered to watch over the entrance. In the front garden a 'For Sale' sign on a stake carried the name of a local estate agent. Dorelia wound down her window.

"I wonder …"

In the passenger seat, Bunty was peering at her phone.

"We should have gone two streets further."

Dorelia executed a neat three-point turn and drove on, but the little tower came with her. She saw its pinkish walls flushed under the pearly, late-winter light, leaf shadows dappling the glass in its narrow windows. As she waited in the clinic's carpark Dorelia saw herself climbing a wooden staircase into the tower. If it were hers, she would set her most comfortable chair beside one of those windows, with a side table for her cup of tea, her pens and papers, and the stacks of books she would read. Dorelia imagined the windows filled with drifting clouds, with birds coasting on air currents, and for the first time since Geordie's death the knot in her chest, which felt as she imagined an overwound clock must feel, relaxed a notch.

When her Geordie died, it had been a shock to come up against that sudden, implacable absence. It was like being slapped hard by an icy hand. Then, in the terrible limbo between his dying and the funeral, she'd caught glimpses of him everywhere, so that coming indoors at dusk, as she reached for the light switch, Geordie's shadow would darken his favourite armchair; in their bedroom, she surprised a flash of his old mustard corduroy coat sleeve in the wardrobe mirror. Every mirror in the house held fragments of Geordie, even the little circular hand-mirror with the crack in it he had used for shaving.

Dorelia would have covered them all with cloths if it hadn't been for the children. They would have pounced on that as a sign that she was not holding up – she imagined Laurence and Hannah frowning and reaching for their phones. Apparently, they stored within those devices lists of suitable places they had researched on their parents' behalf. Retirement settlements and aged care facilities where they – and now Dorelia alone – would feel secure, and where she would be cared for if anything went wrong. By that they meant if she were diagnosed with a serious illness – which was bound to happen at some point – or if her mind began to give way, which was what they expected.

Dorelia knew she sometimes forgot things, but they were usually things she was keen enough to banish – like the name of Hannah's loud and opinionated mother-in-law, or the whereabouts of the personal alarm Laurence had bought and was furious about whenever he turned up and found she wasn't wearing it.

"But Mother, it's in case you FALL."

Since Geordie died, Laurence had taken to shouting at her, perhaps attributing her slow responses to escalating deafness rather than the tightness that ticked and creaked in her chest. But Dorelia heard well enough. And she was not afraid of falling, or not desperately afraid. A lifetime of long walks had kept her reasonably nimble, and she still walked every morning. It kept her mind clear, and even with Geordie's death she had only missed five or six of those early tramps around her neighbourhood route.

For years now, her three adult children had seemed to Dorelia like beloved aliens. If she had not birthed and raised them herself, she would have wondered where they could have sprung from. Geordie hadn't lacked empathy, like Laurence, nor had he been critical and patronising like Hannah. The youngest, Gwenyth, who had been born when Dorelia had thought herself well beyond childbearing, was far kinder than her siblings, but deplorably self-focussed. It puzzled Dorelia that children who'd been as tender as lambs could harden until they were almost unrecognisable. She supposed it was her fault, that she had failed in some vital aspect of childrearing.

The estate agent's name was Pargeter.

"Len," he said, squeezing Dorelia's small dry hand in his large moist mitt. "It's been empty a while," he said. "I suppose it's the sort of place that's gone out of style. Nowadays people prefer new builds."

Dorelia looked around the sitting-room with its open fireplace, and at the kitchen's dated, dark wooden fittings. There was a window above the sink that overlooked a light-washed courtyard; she could put a table and chairs out there and some large terracotta tubs that would be easy to plant up and weed.

"Did you want to see upstairs?" said Len Pargeter.

The wooden staircase was just as she had imagined it, even down to the creak in its second-to-bottom step. But the tower room was lovely beyond anything she could have dreamed – afloat at the level of the treetops, it seemed to Dorelia more like a boat than a room, with everything that might trouble her banished.

"Oh, Mister Pargeter!"

"Len."

"Len," she said, "do you think the owner would consider an offer?"

Len Pargeter grinned and ground his palms together. "No doubt at all," he said. "You just let me have a figure."

# FISH

Leona was leaving them again. Back to Sydney, she said. Whenever this happened Gran or Aunt Nance would arrive and gather up the children, all the while muttering that Sydney was where their flighty mother should have stayed. Leona knew they muttered. Those two had been down on her from the start, she said: nothing she did was ever good enough for them.

From behind the living room curtains Mazz listened as her sister Freddie wept and pleaded with Leona. The twins were out the back under the pergola. Mazz could see them through the smeary window glass, surging back and forth in the dappled light under the grapevine. Skinny legs sticking out of faded shorts, washed-out T-shirts, the boys were oblivious to the storm blowing up inside the house – if their mother left, they might not miss her until bedtime.

Mazz twirled her body more tightly into the rust-coloured chenille curtain. Its weight was like an arm around her nine-year-old shoulders; its dusty cloth smelled of something old and lost she couldn't quite identify. Last time Leona left she had come back after a week, and they'd all got presents. Mazz's was a flower press. Some of the specimens in it were now dry enough to be stuck onto cards. This time their mother would have to take a taxi to the bus station, because the battery in their car was flat.

Mazz considered ringing Aunt Nance to come round and save them, but the telephone was in the hall and Leona would hear. Besides, if she left them there might be another present. Mazz had her heart set on a sable paint brush, but she doubted she'd get one.

Next morning, Freddie gave them their breakfast while Leona nursed the headache she'd had since Aunt Nance – dropping off two dozen eggs from her chooks – had intercepted her climbing into the taxi.

"You might not be much of a mother, Leona," Nance said, "but there's four kids in that house and you're all they've got."

This wasn't strictly true, because there was their father, Sandy. But he was off somewhere driving his truck – as Leona said, "God knows where to."

Nance had snatched the scruffy red vinyl vanity case out of their mother's hand. To the taxi driver, Ray Purdy, she'd jutted her sharp little chin, indicating the boot. Ray had levered himself out from behind the wheel to unload the suitcase and the overnight bag, while Leona, defeated, ran into the house crying and slammed her bedroom door.

It was a relief to get to school. Freddie and Mazz walked there together while Aunt Nance delivered the twins to kindy. Lining up on the dusty asphalt for assembly, marching to their classrooms to the beat of the bass drum and kettle drum, there was a sense of order and predictability to school mornings that Mazz could relax into. She had a spelling test on Mondays, but she wasn't worried; she could read and write much longer words than the ones on the spelling list she hadn't looked at all weekend. Mazz liked school, whereas Freddie hated it. She hated lining up and marching, too, and to avoid it she had put her name down to play the bass drum.

"Frieda Giddings to the front now, please!"

Miss Greaves the music teacher shouted Freddie's name that morning, because with the drama the day before, and doing the breakfast, Freddie must have forgotten it was her turn to play the drum. She hurried forward, flustered, and slipped her arms into the bass drum's wide leather straps.

Freddie was tall and thin like their father, with Sandy's apricot-coloured hair and freckled skin. The bass drum stuck out in front of her like an enormous belly. *Boom. Boom. Boom boom boom.* Mazz had thought of putting her name down to learn the kettle drum so they could play together, but there were too many mornings when she wouldn't be able to concentrate, mornings when she hated their mother. Most of the time, though, she loved her. Because on her good days Leona was the prettiest mother in the town. She was funny, too, though Gran and Aunt Nance could never see that side of her.

Mazz had been drawing in an old scrapbook, had almost filled it, when Aunt Nance announced she was sending her to art classes. "Mazz is artistic," Nance said. "It's a precious gift."

Leona protested about the cost, but Nance was stubborn.

"I'm paying," she said. "Forget the money."

So Mazz went to an art class on Saturday mornings. The teacher was Dutch, from South Africa, a tall, humourless man with faded blue eyes and a turned down mouth. He taught them to draw dull arrangements of fruit and vegetables, sometimes a sheep's skull, always a draped cloth so as to test their skill in rendering the folds.

There was no joy in the classroom. No light. As she laboured over charcoal shadows Mazz wondered why parents sent their kids there, and concluded it was to get them out of the way for a couple of hours while they sat in Giorgio's coffee lounge, smoking, and drinking cappuccinos.

There was a day when they were asked to draw something from a newspaper and add their own touches to it. One girl drew a portrait of a woman – a goddess with parted lips and perfect eyebrows – and altered it by adding a nun's veil. When the teacher saw it, he spoke coldly.

"Who is responsible for this blasphemy?"

The class went quiet. When the girl whose drawing it was put up her hand, Mazz had thought the teacher was going to strike her.

"Out! Out! Out!" he screamed, fury igniting in his pale blue eyes.

The girl cowered as he hustled her to the door. Afterwards it was whispered that she had copied a portrait of Christine Keeler. Mazz's parents never bought newspapers. She didn't know who Christine Keeler was, or why drawing her had made the teacher angry. The girl never came back to the class.

At school Mazz came top in most of her subjects. She was smart, Aunt Nance said. People in the town agreed that Mazz had got the brains and Freddie had got the looks, and it was true that Freddie, at thirteen, with her long slim legs and spill of strawberry blonde hair, was striking. But there was a sharpness to her nose and mouth, and her glorious hair was too often dulled with hairspray. Whereas beneath Mazz's dormouse demeanor, her unruly brown curls, she had copped Leona's bone structure. Hers was to be a slow release of beauty.

The school principal and Aunt Nance arranged for Mazz to sit the entrance exam for a boarding school in Adelaide. When Mazz won a full scholarship, Leona threw a fit about her going away, but Gran and Aunt Nance prevailed.

"You can't hold her back, Leona," Nance said.

The twins Don and Jonty were in primary school, and Freddie was only hanging on at high school until she was old enough to leave. Mazz had read Enid Blyton's books and was anticipating midnight feasts and other adventures, while Leona muttered darkly that if Mazz went to the city she would never come home. She was talking nonsense, as usual, Nance said. Of course she'd come home, every school holiday, but Leona shook her head. There were tears in her eyes, and years later, when Mazz had not only left the town but Australia, she would recall her mother's prediction and be amazed at her prescience.

Those first school holidays, Mazz stepped off the Adelaide bus to a flurry of attention. Everyone who saw her exclaimed at how much she had grown. But within hours, the family had adjusted to make room for her again, and soon it felt as if boarding school was a place she had dreamed. No one wanted to talk about it; it was as if she had never gone away. The town, though, let Mazz know that there was something different about her now. Women came to the door asking for Leona, and when Mazz didn't know why they'd come the women's eyebrows would draw together, and they'd tilt their heads at her in a way that said maybe she wasn't as sharp as they'd thought. It transpired that in her absence Leona had taken up op-shopping and re-selling. The house was choked with her stock and in the late afternoons it filled with a steady trickle of customers.

Freddie had a crush on Ryan Barry and was absorbed with waiting for him to ring, or to take her somewhere. The old closeness between the sisters, the united front they had always presented to Leona, and to the rest of the world, had been breached by an apprentice fitter and turner at the zinc mine. Ryan would arrive in the early evening, hair wet-combed into a quiff, and carry Freddie off to the drive-in, or to one of the town's many watering holes. Only the twins were the same, shyly hugging her when she first arrived, after which she was ignored. All their waking hours were spent kicking and bouncing balls, and in the fortnight she was at home they broke two windows.

It was the long Christmas holiday when Mazz announced that she had gone vegetarian. Not only that, but there was to be no more 'Mazz'; the nickname was childish, it was an embarrassment, and she would like them to call her by her proper name, Mariel. She asked her sister why she put up with a boy's stupid nickname and insisted on addressing her as Frieda.

Mazz had gone all la-de-dah on them, Freddie said, and the two boys laughed and circled Mazz, chanting: "La de dah, lah de dah!"

Leona, to Mazz's surprise, told them all to leave her alone.

"I picked those names," she said, "and it's about time youse girls started using them."

They were Sydney names, Mariel suspected, but didn't ask. Like the boys, she was silenced by their mother's challenging stare.

"This bloody town," Leona muttered.

But Leona had chosen to marry their father, Mariel reasoned. When Sandy had proposed, she could have said no. Freddie loyally stuck up for the town whenever their mother ran it down, though like the rest of them she was awed by the yellowed newspaper clippings that showed Leona arriving from Sydney to model in the spring dress parades at Pellew and Moore. And then, off duty at the picnic races, her platinum curls and wriggling walk had caught the eye of Sandy Giddings.

All their father's friends had warned him she'd be trouble, Aunt Nance said. But Sandy hadn't listened. Sometimes Leona would tell the story of their courtship with a giggle in her voice, but when things were going wrong none of them would risk reminding her, as their Aunt Nance did, that she had made her bed and now she'd have to lie in it.

When Leona cooked vegetarian lasagne for the first time, they all ate it, though the boys, behind her back, made vomiting gestures. It was that Christmas that Mariel noticed the lack of proper footpaths in their street, the absence of a kerb, or trees, anything civilising. She saw, too, that their old house was shabby, despite Leona's efforts with shade cloth and sword ferns. From the street, blinds and curtains drawn against the sun, it crouched sulkily in its own dusty shade, its mood reminding Mariel of their mother getting over one of her blowups. White ants had undermined the shed where Sandy stored his tools and were making inroads into the back veranda. Their father was supposed to have got the pest control people in before his last trip, Leona said, but they'd never turned up.

Even Aunt Nance's house, though neat inside, had cracked tiles and peeling paintwork. In its backyard, a ramshackle row of hutches housed the rabbits she and her son Dale bred to eat. The sight of creatures she had once pleaded to be allowed to pet struck Mariel now as gruesome, a sad death row that somehow stood for the town. Their Gran's place, where they had spent so much time as children, was nearly derelict. In her spidery sleepout, with its concrete floor that had never had lino on it, or a rug, its iron beds and ancient wardrobes were furred with dust. But however decrepit that house became, Mariel could never bring herself to hate it. Watching her Gran feed kindling into her wood stove stirred memories of Christmases and birthdays, Gran cooking for them because Leona was having a fit. Mariel had learned to iron handkerchiefs at the kitchen table, and she still knew where everything belonged in the drawers and cupboards from helping with the washing up.

But at home now the op-shop clothes had spilled over into the bathroom, at times even dangling from the shower rail. They had migrated into Mariel's wardrobe, and she was relieved when it was time to return to school.

After boarding school, Mariel funded her courses at the Central School of Art with waitressing and cleaning jobs. She had a room in a big, rundown share house at Glenelg, and the trips home became fewer. In their place there were long telephone calls with Freddie, who was getting engaged to Ryan Barry.

"You'll come home for the party, won't you?" Freddie said.

"Of course. When is it?"

"As soon as Ryan pays off the ring."

"How's Leona?"

"Too thin. I'm worried about her."

"She's never been fat."

"No, but never like this. I mean, she's got the body of a sixteen-year-old."

"Well, half her luck," Mariel said. "At her age, a sixteen-year-old body is something most women can only dream of."

One rainy night there was a frantic tapping at Mariel's window. It was a woman from her life drawing class. Diana's hair was wet, her clothes flung on anyhow, and she had lost her shoes. With her face blotchy from crying, she told Mariel she had run away from her husband. He'd hit her again and she'd been afraid that this time he was really going to hurt her. Mariel put her arms around the shivering woman. She made hot chocolate, and when Diana's teeth had stopped chattering, she improvised a bed for her on the floor. This arrangement lasted for weeks, Diana repaying Mariel's kindness by cleaning and tidying the house, until a room became vacant and she moved in with her belongings.

Mariel had always known that men would use their fists against women, that they could terrify them into running barefoot from their houses in the middle of the night. Her own father hadn't been violent, but there were plenty in the town who were. Ray Purdy had broken his wife's arm once over something she'd cooked, yet people were reluctant to interfere between a husband and wife. In the street, or at the supermarket, women with bruised arms and blackened eyes behind sunglasses dared you to look at them.

Leona had never forgotten the murder that had happened the year she arrived in the town, when a girl of seventeen, Flora Helsden, had gone to a dance and was found dead the next morning on the oval.

"That could so easily have been me," Leona said.

This was what could happen to girls who went off into the dark with men. Leona was mainly warning Freddie, but later she would make sure that Mariel knew about Flora.

Diana's brother, a lawyer, was helping with her divorce. As soon as she got her settlement, she was going overseas.

"Karl is furious he's had to buy me out of the house. I want to get away before he boils over again." She was going to London. "Why don't you come too?"

Mariel had some savings, but she was planning to finish out her year at the art school. Yet it stirred her, watching Diana plan her escape, and the glamour of Europe was an undeniable pull. She was tempted, but resisted, much to Diana's disappointment, for the two had become close these last months, even though Diana, at thirty, seemed old to Mariel.

Freddie's engagement party was held at the end of February. There was to be a formal celebration in the function room of a hotel on the Saturday night, jointly hosted by Leona and Sandy, and Ryan Barry's parents. Freddie sent Mariel a photograph of her dress and shoes inside the invitation card and warned that on the Friday night there was to be a private party at home.

It had already kicked off by the time Mariel got off the bus. Leona had strung fairy lights under the pergola. Mosquito coils smoked in the pots of sun-scorched ferns that lined the patio, and Sandy had fired up the barbecue. Freddie was flashing her engagement ring. She wore a lime green dress that made her freckles stand out, and her hair hung in an exhausted orange wave over one shoulder. When her mother emerged from the kitchen Mariel could barely conceal her surprise: Leona had lost a startling amount of weight and her body was indeed that of a slight teen. She was wearing a teen's clothing, too, gleaned from her op-shop stash: a pink gingham halter-neck top and a tiny denim skirt embroidered with rhinestone butterflies. There were matching butterfly clips in her hair, which was drawn into schoolgirl bunches on either side of her smoking-ravaged face. Purple shadows, like bruises, lay beneath her eyes, and Leona's too-pale pink lipstick had slipped off the corners of her mouth; she was sucking on one of her interminable mints.

"Hello, Darl! You got here in one piece, then."

When Leona hugged her, Mariel felt her mother's bird-like bones.

Sandy had rigged up a bar, and there was a keg of beer. He lounged beside it in his shorts and a short-sleeved shirt, looking as he did at the races, or the dogs – full of laddish good-humour, expectant, ready to enjoy himself. He'd got the two boys looking after the barbecue, and he showed Mariel the Weber where he was cooking a whole fish wrapped in foil.

Mariel wasn't hungry, and she was still vegetarian, though everyone, including Leona, seemed to have forgotten. A clutch of Freddie's friends arrived and put on music. Mariel looked around for somewhere to sit, as a Neil Diamond song she particularly disliked blared from a small speaker. One of the twins swooped by on a skateboard, lanky inside baggy clothing, taller now even than Freddie. All that night, and for the rest of her visit, Mariel felt the two boys as shadows flitting past her in the dark, while her sister was like a wind-up doll, showing her ring over and over, standing with one arm around Ryan's neck as if she would dangle there for the rest of her life.

Mariel was glad she hadn't brought Diana. It had been a near miss – Diana had been at a loose end and had floated the idea of coming. But at the last minute one of their housemates had invited her to an exhibition opening and the after party. Mariel sweated at the thought of what Diana, with her raw silk sheath dresses and beautiful narrow shoes, would have made of the town and her family.

When the fish was cooked to Sandy's satisfaction, the foil parcel was transferred to a big oval serving platter; it was put in the middle of a picnic table and the foil peeled back. Everyone gathered round. Mariel had an impression of charred, silvery skin, a dull shimmer. Sandy stood beside it, beaming, and Mariel wondered what kind of fish it was. Someone had said, but she hadn't been able to hold the information. Keeping hold of anything was impossible. The lightbulb on a corner of the patio threw down a cone of cold white light in which dozens of small moths flapped and jittered. With the smell of the food, the smoke from the barbecue, and the heat radiating from bricks and concrete, Mariel felt queasy; her head began to throb.

It was Ryan Barry who leaned in first and cut into the fish. With Freddie still dangling from his muscular brown neck, he picked up a piece in his fingers and pushed it into his mouth.

"Mmmm, it's good, all right," Ryan said.

At that, Freddie plucked at it with her free hand, and the twins dived into the foil and their fingers came out holding lumps of fish. Leona's sliver left an oily smear across her chin. Freddie's friends joined in, it was all hands now, tearing at the fish. Sandy pulled off a big piece and retreated to the barbecue. Mouthful by mouthful, the fish was stripped of its flesh, and the hands and faces glistened with grease and with the fish's juices. Under the harsh patio light, there were dozens more moths.

Mariel hurried into the house and locked the bathroom door. Even Van Gogh's potato eaters in their poor, rustic kitchen had used cutlery. They might have been peasants, their bodies distorted by crushing labour, but they had taken coffee in tiny white cups, they had shown basic courtesy, and table manners. Mariel thought of paintings of people sharing food, and could think of none in which hands had grabbed and stripped, and mouths had gobbled.

Leona's stock had been cleared from the bathroom for the party, but the musty, smoky stink of old clothing still clung to the shower curtain, to the bath mat and the towels, in spite of the chemical air freshener.

It was then, sitting on the closed toilet lid, that Mariel made up her mind to go overseas with Diana. She could defer her courses and work and study in London. It was impossible to guess what her future might look like in another country, but she had known since schooldays that she could not stay in the town, like Freddie. Tonight, even Adelaide did not feel far enough away; it did not feel safe. There was still a chance that some loose thread of loyalty, some inescapable filament of duty, might hook her. Then she would be trapped here, thrashing with distress.

More people were arriving. Mariel heard the slam of car doors, heavy footsteps, shouted greetings over the inevitable Abba track. She thought of Flora Helsden who had gone to a dance, and fought for her life, and lost, on the football oval. She had never got away from the town. But why was she even thinking of that poor dead girl now, at her sister's engagement party?

Mariel stood up and stared at herself in the mirror, at her prim black dress and unpierced ears, her slender, ringless fingers. She was filled with grief that she belonged to this place and an almost equal grief that she could never truly belong. Because the town, with its broad, dust-blasted streets, though so intimately known, could never be real to her. It was not Abba she wanted, but some music she had not yet heard, music scored for violins, a cello, for other instruments she could not name. Her dreams were filled with white damask-covered tables lit by candles, with garden flowers loosely arranged in slender vases. Surely there was no man here tonight who could entice her out into the dark as Ryan Barry had enticed her sister. If that ever happened she would be ruined, like poor Freddie, who was so far gone as to not even know she was gone.

*Fish*

Within weeks Mariel was plunged into the chill beauty of an English spring. In London's daffodil-studded parks the breeze carried a breath of the countryside's cool green abundance, while pale blossom starred the slender branches spread against old stone walls. Glowing inside the cherry wool coat she had bought in the sales at Selfridges, Mariel returned again and again to the National Gallery and the Tate, to stare at paintings she had only ever seen as reproductions. Afterwards, she would walk beside the Thames, clutching the postcards she'd bought in the gallery shop.

It was already dark when she returned one afternoon to the rooms she shared with Diana in a semi-detached house in Hendon. She was still buoyed by the wonder of Whistler's muted masterpieces when she found a letter waiting for her on the hall table. It was from Freddie. They should have guessed about Leona's weight loss, Freddie said. Their mother had flown to Adelaide for tests without telling anyone; she'd never told them the results. And now she flatly refused all treatment, refused even to give up smoking. *There's no point in coming home, Mazz, she'll be gone before you can book a flight.*

Leona was leaving them. This time she was going for good. Mariel propped the Whistler postcards on the windowsill, delight erased by the memory of her mother's bones and by the presence of the town that leapt out at her from her sister's letter – its huddled houses, its heat-beaten streets, its backyards riddled with caged, doomed animals. Mariel flung herself down on her bed and covered her face with the pillow. Her family, the town: she felt their insistent pull and her own cornered, panicky resistance.

Another letter came after Leona's funeral. *I had no idea she knew so many people.* Freddie was pregnant, and their mother had known she would not live to see her first grandchild. *You were her sun moon and stars, though, Mazz. She said at the end, that when she was young in Sydney, she had wanted to be a girl just like you.*

If Ryan Barry had not paid off the engagement ring.
If Diana had never knocked on her window.
If their father had not barbecued a fish.

In the days that followed, Mariel returned to stand for a long time in front of Whistler's paintings. In her cherry coat, her hair a dark cloud floating against grey and blue-green walls, she herself presented a picture that others passing through the gallery turned to gaze at with awe. Before Whistler's girl in white, with her beautiful sleeves and her fan, Mariel's eyes filled with tears. She wished she could have shown it to Leona – not a reproduction, but the real thing.

When she had looked at the paintings for so long that her eyes began to droop with tiredness, she made her way to Selfridges, and there, over tea and a sandwich in the late afternoon lull, she filled in a job application for a hotel receptionist's position. If she got it, it would be a pity to leave London, to move away from the places where she might have studied. But everything was more expensive than she'd bargained for, and her funds were dwindling. Mariel slipped the paperwork into an envelope, and as she was leaving the store a clock somewhere struck the hour, silvery notes soaring like arrows into the darkening sky. Oxford Street was crowded with people hurrying home from work; it was nearly night, and the day was already past.

# THE TOWER

It was Dorelia's great good fortune to have stumbled upon the tower house during a rare window of inattention from her children. Laurence's engineering firm had sent him to establish a new office in Berlin, and his wife and daughter had gone with him to 'do Europe'. Before they left they had planned a sightseeing itinerary that to Dorelia sounded exhausting; it was to finish up with a cruise on the Rhine. Meanwhile, Hannah had begun a semester of study leave, and she was spending part of it at the Alexander Turnbull Library in Wellington, where she was to examine their Katherine Mansfield collection. Gwenyth had not gone away, but it would transpire that she had fallen in love. Loved up and senseless, she had become deaf dumb and blind to the world and especially to her mother.

Dorelia asked Len Pargeter if he would convey her offer to the owner of the tower house and handle the sale, by auction, of her home. Len rubbed his palms together so briskly and for so long that Dorelia felt a snap of electricity when he shook her hand.

"Of course, dear lady, consider it done!"

After three open inspections, the house where Dorelia had passed the bulk of her long marriage was sold at auction on a sunny Saturday afternoon to an insurance executive with a young family. Dorelia was pleased that there would once again be small children playing in the garden, and that the empty bedrooms, which had often spooked her at night, would soon be occupied.

The only person she had told of her plan to buy the tower house was Bunty. After more than half a century of friendship, Bunty's discretion could be relied upon: Bunty was staunch. Dorelia's boldness in moving house without consulting her children had drawn no criticism from her friend, only offers of help and a wistful enquiry as to whether she would be able to manage the tower's stairs with her stick when she visited. Dorelia had assured her that she was having a handrail fitted before she moved in.

"And what will you do up there in your stronghold?" Bunty was biting into one of the cinnamon doughnuts the two of them drove across town on Thursday mornings to buy from the place they called 'the good bakery'.

Dorelia poured their tea. "I'll read," she said.

Bunty nodded, and her left hand trembled, slopping tea into the saucer. They both ignored this lapse, while she switched the cup to her right hand, her painting hand, which was as firm as ever.

"These doughnuts are especially good today!" Dorelia said.

With her long, iron-coloured hair bundled at the nape of her neck, Bunty's profile reminded Dorelia of Virginia Woolf's, only of course she had lived far longer than Virginia had managed. Dorelia watched her friend brush sugar from her lips with the back of one long, age-freckled hand and the grace of this gesture triggered an ache of nostalgia: Bunty's hands had always been beautiful, and in a time that was far behind them Dorelia had made dozens of charcoal studies of her friend's hands and feet. They had modelled for each other all through art school, and beyond. Oh, those years! Sometimes Dorelia longed for them so fiercely that she'd have done anything, struck any bargain, to have them back.

What if there was a way to dissolve the border between past and present, she mused. What if there was a portal through which the deep past could still be accessed – would she enter back into that time, when the two of them had been young, and she had dreamed of devoting herself to art rather than to a husband and children? Going back, might there be the chance to do things differently? Dorelia drew a slow, resigned breath and felt the familiar ache in her chest: even now, if such a thing were possible, she couldn't not choose Geordie.

"I will write, too," she said.

"You should never have abandoned your memoir."

Dorelia had finished her first doughnut and was wondering whether she should save the second for when her energy levels dipped in the late afternoon. "Not the memoir," she said. "At least, not for the moment."

Bunty pulled a face. "Do you mean to say you're going to allow our wonder years to be ploughed under into the great nothingness?"

"It's been so long since I wrote anything." Dorelia's eyes grew wistful, and she reached for the second doughnut. "I thought I'd get my hand in first with something subversive."

Bunty rocked forward in her chair and clapped, two sharp smacks, a familiar gesture of approval. She raised her eyebrows, or the place on her high pale forehead where her eyebrows had once been two beautiful dark arcs. The thinning of their brows made old women's faces look naked, thought Dorelia, although it threw the emphasis back onto their eyes, and her friend's delicately moulded, deeply set, prune-black eyes, were lit with enthusiasm.

Where would she be without this friendship, Dorelia wondered? A shiver went through her whenever she thought about which of them would die first. Selfishly she hoped she would go before her friend, but on the other hand it gutted her to think of Bunty alone.

Bunty was waiting, doughnut poised, for Dorelia to explain.

"I thought I'd re-write the stories that put old women in a poor light," Dorelia said.

"But where will you start? There are so many."

"I'm going to begin with Rapunzel's witch. I mean, which reader of *Grimm's Fairy Tales* has been left with even a smidgeon of sympathy for her?"

Bunty gave a snorting laugh. "She suffers from childless-woman syndrome," she said. "I'll be cheering you on if you can redeem the poor creature."

Dorelia patted Bunty's hand that wasn't holding the doughnut, depositing a glitter of sticky sugar. They had often discussed the suspicion that attached to childless women; it was ages-old, a malign and subtle social undercurrent. Even now, when many women were childless by choice, you could still rub up against that prejudice, though at Bunty's age it tended to manifest as pity. People wondered, at times intrusively, who would look after her when she went gaga, usually with an ominous reference to the lack of a daughter. Dorelia was able to console Bunty on this score with the long-held certainty that neither of her daughters would be much use to her if a time came when she could no longer manage. The girls did love her, each in their own way, and they would probably try to help. But Dorelia couldn't imagine either of them as a willing carer; more to the point, she could not imagine herself being cared for by them.

"I'll re-frame her story," Dorelia said, "to show that Rapunzel's witch was misunderstood."

"I have always thought about the Rapunzel story," said Bunty, "that it can be read as a type of surrogacy contract. The witch is too old to conceive, so she transfers her longing to the young, pregnant wife, focussing her desire on the green leaves of the rampion."

Dorelia stayed silent. This was a painful topic for Bunty, and perhaps she should have said she was going to re-write another tale. After all, centuries of storytelling had left plenty to choose from.

"When the baby is born, she is given to the witch," Bunty said. "But isn't it strange that once Rapunzel's parents have parted with their child, nothing more is heard of them?" Bunty raised her face to her friend, her eyes momentarily bleak. "I believe there's a version in which the parents later set off fireworks to encourage their grown-up daughter to come home. But yes, in the story most often told, it is as if they were nothing but a gateway."

Dorelia nodded, and after a while said, "It's true, they slip so quickly from the page that a reader must suspect the point of view. Is it really the witch in control, relegating the biological parents to mere donors of egg and sperm, privileging nurture over nature?"

They were startled by the telephone. It was Hannah, an eerily clear connection from Wellington, ringing to check that her mother was all right.

Dorelia closed her eyes and drew a deep breath. "I'm fine, darling. But you ought to know, I have sold the house."

It seemed an age before Dorelia was able to speak again. Hannah supposed she had been taken advantage of by some predatory real estate salesman, or even a straight-out con man. Or she'd had a breakdown; she was hallucinating. But surely it was not too late to undo whatever mad thing she had agreed to? At last there was a small silence and Dorelia spoke into it with relief.

"No, the cooling off period is over," she said. "It's a done deal."

# KANDAHAR

"That boy will be the death of us!"

Aldith's mother would exclaim this often throughout her grandson's childhood, always with a doting laugh. And Aldith, helplessly smitten since she had first laid eyes upon her son's crumpled, newborn face, would answer with an indulgent smile. The two women watched fondly as Jack swung himself up onto a branch of the cherry tree in the garden of Mrs Cunningham's ground-floor Maida Vale flat, or raced his bicycle along the pathways in the park. Grazed elbows and knees did not deter him, nor even the odd broken bone. Aldith and her mother thought Jack's daring admirable, if at times a little heart-stopping.

Ten years after Jack was born, Aldith would marry and give birth to two more sons. Holding first Charlie and later Aaron, she would be flooded with joy, but with Jack there had been more than joy. Jack had brought with him a feeling of the world cracked open, a sensation Aldith identified as bliss. Perhaps the depth of her feelings for her eldest child sprang from the fact that when he was born, she had been young and single. Raising Jack had given her a purpose at a time when she had been fumbling forward in the dark.

Jack was the child of a man Aldith had worked for in her first job after leaving school. She had been staying with an aunt in

St Leonards one Easter, when she had spotted the advertisement for a 'Girl Friday' in the *Bexhill Observer.* Looking back, she could see that it had been natural at eighteen to long for a breathing space. Even though in the Maida Vale flat there was only her and her mother, Dora, Aldith had been feeling crowded and restless. School life had been regimented and busy; its final years had required unusual endurance. A few girls Aldith knew would go on to university, but most had been looking for their first jobs. Aldith had done well enough, but the prospect of returning to stuffy classrooms was unbearable, and Dora – although not openly opposed to further study – had looked visibly relieved when Aldith decided against it.

Since the death of her father, Aldith had been tied to her mother. Dora was a docile, undemanding woman, but their perpetual closeness, and the flat with its William Morris-papered rooms, its ornaments that were dusted once a week and returned to the same positions, had become irksome to Aldith. Her Aunt Ida was a vague, slightly scatty spinster whose only interest in life appeared to be painting in watercolours, yet she had divined her niece's desire to escape and had encouraged her to consider her options.

"You're only young once," Ida said, pouring tea for them from a blue and white teapot. "So you might as well spread your wings."

Later, alone in the kitchen, Aldith had found the local newspaper folded open to the Situations Vacant.

Victor Maddingly was in his late thirties or early forties; dark-haired, dark-eyed, he exuded a restless energy. At the interview he wore a white collarless shirt with a turquoise scarf knotted at his throat. On his wrist was a thin silver bracelet etched with Arabic script. At first Aldith had supposed he must be an artist, or an actor.

Victor ran an import business. He explained that Aldith would often be alone in the office. Besides himself, there were two storemen, but they had their own office at the rear of the warehouse.

"Do you think you are up to it?" he said. "You won't be lonely?"

Aldith had said that as an only child she was accustomed to spending time alone, although when she had been shown the dusty room with its ancient safe, its filing cabinets, and the scarred wooden desk where she would sit to answer the telephone, to sort the mail, and type Victor Maddingly's letters, she had wondered whether she should keep on sifting through the newspaper.

"This is where you will hold the fort when I'm away, which I'm afraid will be rather often."

Aldith nodded. It meant that for much of the time she would be her own boss and this appealed to her in her present mood.

"Your predecessor is calling in tomorrow to return her keys," Victor Maddingly said. "I can ask her to give you a quick run-down of the office routines and duties."

So Aldith had telephoned Dora and told her she was taking a job in Hastings.

"It'll be good experience," she said, ignoring the wobble in her mother's voice, pushing away the image of her slight figure standing in the hall beside the telephone on its narrow table.

"Oh, absolutely!" Dora's voice echoed in the empty flat.

Aldith started work the following day, bringing with her a bag of dusters and a can of spray polish from her aunt's, where she would stay until her first wages enabled her to rent her own place.

The outgoing secretary, Anna, was tall and thin, with a twist of pale blonde hair held in place by a tortoiseshell clip. Her long, narrow face was wary as she greeted Aldith, yet she laughed when she spotted the dusters and the polish.

"You'll be wasting your time," she said. "In summer the trucks coming in and out stir up the dust and in winter the condensation sets it like concrete."

"What do the trucks deliver?" Aldith had forgotten to ask this in her interview.

"Rugs and textiles, mainly, from Iran, Afghanistan, India, Morocco. Victor travels three or four times a year on buying trips, though less often now to Afghanistan."

Something about the way Victor Maddingly's first name fell so softly from Anna's lips made Aldith glance up sharply. Anna fumbled in her handbag and produced a bunch of keys.

"The three smaller ones are for the filing cabinets and this square one unlocks the front door. Victor, Mr Maddingly, doesn't usually appear until around ten."

From the few letters she had already seen, Aldith knew that V. R. Maddingly & Co. supplied many of London's upmarket interior designers and even some dealers in Europe. All from this shabby, high-ceilinged office, with its worn linoleum, its stunted aspidistra, and the tall, frosted glass windows that on inspection she found to be painted shut. When she expressed her surprise at this dinginess to Anna, the other girl shrugged.

"Victor is generous in some ways, though never with himself. He believes in looking after the pennies. I don't think he'll ever redecorate."

As she was leaving, Anna had lingered in the doorway. "Well, I hope you'll be happy," she said.

And then she was gone, leaving Aldith alone in the silent office with its diffused, underwater light.

From the start, Victor Maddingly seemed oblivious to the usual distance that existed between employer and employee. He would perch on a corner of her desk to dictate a letter, screwing up his face in concentration while she sat with her fingers poised above the keyboard. In another sort of man this might have worried Aldith, but Victor exuded conviviality and, as Anna had said, generosity. If he made himself a cup of tea, he always brought one to Aldith. On Fridays he would send her out to the bakery for cakes and insist they share them. She understood that it was his nature to be friendly, and there were only the two of them in the office.

Sometimes, as they sat together over tea and sponge cake, he would tell her about the places he visited on his buying expeditions. Listening to him, Aldith saw the crowded souks, with their snake charmers, their wandering storytellers and musicians, their shopkeepers proffering glasses of sweet mint tea.

"Please, call me Victor," he said, towards the end of the second week. "Whenever I hear Mr Maddingly it makes me think my father has just arrived, and he died some years ago."

"Was it your father's business?" Aldith asked.

"Yes, the old man was a natural dealer, and he had the right contacts."

When Aldith mentioned that she had moved into a bedsitter, Victor asked if she was all right for furniture.

"I've taken it furnished," she said.

Victor nodded. "A dreary, mismatched collection, if I know anything about those houses."

"It is a bit on the gloomy side," Aldith admitted.

To her surprise, he plunged into the store behind the office and reappeared holding a rolled-up rug.

"Throw this on your floor," he said. "It'll cheer the place up." He spread the rug on the lino at their feet.

"Oh, it's lovely! But I can't afford it."

Victor waved away her protest. "Take it! It's an awkward size and I'd rather it adorned your bedsit than lie around here gathering dust." He rolled it up again and secured it with string. "It was woven in Kandahar," he said, pressing the bundle into her arms.

Late one Friday afternoon after they'd been working on stocktaking lists, Victor Maddingly had invited her to supper.

"There is a bistro I like called Proust's, only I don't feel in the mood to eat alone."

There was a boyish wistfulness about him, and Aldith thought she recognised the look of someone who dreaded returning to an empty house and a solitary dinner. Now that the novelty of having her own bedsit had worn off, she often felt the same, particularly on a Friday evening. So, she fetched her coat, and they walked together through the winding streets of the Old Town.

It was early autumn and already dark. Stepping carefully over the cobbles of the lane that led to Proust's, Aldith had a sense of herself that was brand new – she was an independent girl, almost nineteen, with smooth olive skin and soft dark hair; a girl with a slender, fine-boned body, and a face in which the best features of her individually attractive parents had come to rest in a form that was uniquely her own. And this smoothly formed girl was strolling towards a restaurant in the company of an older but still-attractive man, chatting to him as calmly as if she always did this sort of thing, when in fact it was a first.

At the restaurant, the chef came out of the kitchen to greet Victor; it appeared the two were old friends. The menu was in French, and Aldith let Victor order for both of them. As they lingered over the wine, he entertained her with an account of the last trip he'd made to Kandahar.

"Old Kandahar was laid out by Alexander the Great in 330 BC," he said, "and destroyed in 1738 by Nadir Shah Afshar of Persia." He described how its ancient, rose-coloured ruins loomed out of the desert, how in the honeyed light of that place it shimmered like a fairy tale palace. Even now, at the top of its fortified citadel, he said, were the remains of royal apartments.

As Victor spoke, the skin on Aldith's neck and arms began to tingle; there was warmth in her chest, which she put down to the wine. Ordinary life fell away, and what was left was as richly patterned as the rugs and textiles he bargained for in these far-flung places.

Afterwards, Victor walked her back to her bedsit. That was the beginning, and all she had asked as he unknotted his turquoise scarf was whether he was married. He had assured her he was not. At work, it had not been awkward, as she had feared it might be. After all, there was no one to remark that their body language had become less formal, or to notice if Victor dropped a kiss on her hair as he passed through the office. His own office was a cluttered cubbyhole off the store. It suited him, he said, to keep an eye on the drivers and the storemen as they loaded and unloaded his treasures.

Most Friday evenings they returned to Proust's, or they ordered a bar meal in one of the Old Town's dimly lit pubs. From there, mellow with wine, with coffee and brandy, they would walk to Aldith's bedsit. Once, when the weather was particularly foul, Victor brought his car and said he'd take her to his place for a glass of champagne. He was leaving the following day on one of his buying trips, so it was to be a farewell celebration.

He lived in St Leonards in a tall, red brick Victorian house on a quiet street not far from Aunt Ida's. It had belonged to his parents. The front door was the same turquoise as Victor's favourite neckerchief, and inside it was an eclectic mix of French and English antiques mingled with the wall hangings, carvings, and carpets, that Victor and his father before him had collected on their travels. Aldith looked around curiously while he poured their drinks. Even though she had believed him about not being married, it was reassuring to find that he lived alone and in a style that was more orderly than she had imagined.

Victor's bed was a dark four-poster, with a carved headboard and pale muslin curtains. He'd had it shipped in pieces from Bali and reassembled in the bedroom.

"You'd love it in Bali," he said, running a finger down the slope of Aldith's cheekbone to her chin.

Looking into his eyes, Aldith had allowed herself to wonder whether he might take her there one day, or to Kandahar to see the ruins of the old citadel. Victor had drawn the bed curtains but left the windows open, so that moonlight filtered through the muslin and turned the sheets and their bodies silver. Already, in her mind, Victor was far away, he was riding a camel towards Old Kandahar, or he was sipping mint tea in the desert with a Berber carpet merchant. Jack was conceived in the Balinese bed.

When Aldith married Matthew Ledwidge at a London registry office, she wore a cream linen dress that was already creased by the time she left her mother's flat. She carried a bouquet of red rosebuds and Queen Anne's lace, which she and Jack had gone together to collect from the florist. After the ceremony, their small wedding party walked to a pub with a garden overlooking the canal – the bride and groom hand in hand, Aldith's mother and Jack, and Matthew's friend Paul with Sinead, his Irish girlfriend.

Aldith was filled with pride at the sight of her son's spotless white shirt, the bright tie she had chosen for him – it was his first suit, and he wore a red rosebud pinned to his lapel. Jack was dark-haired, with eyes of an arresting green, and it was Dora's often expressed opinion, with which Aldith could only agree, that he would break more than a few hearts once he reached his teens.

The afternoon was fine, with the scent of summer flowers and cut grass wafting across the water. As the newlyweds were toasted with champagne, Aldith could not have been happier. She smiled at Matthew and Jack, sitting close, with matching buttonholes. Victor Maddingly had never been part of their lives, and when her pregnancy had begun to show, Aldith had returned to live with her mother. Dora had embraced the arrangement, with never a scolding word about her daughter's single motherhood. She had been a second mother to Jack, and the two had always been close. But now there was Matthew, and to Aldith's relief he had from the first treated Jack as his own. She was not yet thirty: they would have other children.

Charlie and Aaron were four and five when the bank Matt worked for offered him a posting outside London.

"It's a promotion," Aldith explained to her mother. "We don't have a choice."

The county they found themselves in was dotted with market towns and villages built from honey-coloured stone. There were picture-book high streets, and eventually, outside Malmesbury, they found an affordable cottage surrounded by fields and hedgerows and within easy driving distance of Matt's office. There was a walnut tree at the back and a rose-smothered fence in front. Aldith spent that autumn studying copies of *Country Living* magazine for decorating ideas and planning a cottage garden. She took the children to pick blackberries and rosehips in the hedgerows and persuaded Matt that they should keep hens. The hen house became his first building project.

Jack was the only one, aside from Dora, who had been dismayed by the prospect of them leaving London. It was the change of school he resisted and the loss of his friends.

Aldith had tried to console him.

"You can stay at Gran's some weekends," she said. "And you'll make new friends here."

She looked up into Jack's green-gold eyes, their colour always reminding her of the Afghan rug Victor had given her all those years ago. Jack was taller than her now and passing through that period of soft, almost feminine beauty that young men inhabit in the fleeting interval between boyhood and manhood. Jack was beautiful, but he was touchy, especially about the country.

"There's nothing to do," he said. "It's so boring."

He refused to go blackberrying, or to join them on walks; he was a silent presence in their midst, and in desperation Aldith suggested to Matt that they should get Jack a dog to help him settle.

Matt wasn't keen on the dog. "It's just a phase. He'll get over it."

Since the move, Jack and Matt had been tense around each other. Jack's discontent was a bass note pulsing beneath their daily lives, and anything could set him off and start a row. Aldith hoped he would soon make new friends and that they would all be happy again, as they had been in London. In an effort to integrate into the local community she joined a choir, and there she met Julia Swift. The two quickly became friends.

Like Aldith, Julia had moved because of her husband's work; she had given up a job she'd loved in an advertising agency in Edinburgh. Her husband Simon was an architect who specialised in the conservation and restoration of historic buildings.

"He's working on a huge old National Trust wreck that's going to keep him busy for years."

The two couples lived within cycling distance of each other. They socialised at weekends, taking turns to host dinner parties, and sometimes on a Sunday, mildly hung-over, they would gather the children and go for long country walks. Julia and Simon had a five-year-old daughter, Mollie, and were deciding whether they would have more children. Julia was resisting, but Simon was adamant.

"You can't let Mollie be an only child," he said. "It isn't fair."

"I was an only child," Aldith protested. "I never minded."

Julia rolled her eyes whenever the subject came up, though privately she told Aldith that she would probably capitulate.

The two couples had booked to dine in a French restaurant in the town to celebrate Aldith and Matt's wedding anniversary. At the last minute, Aldith wasn't able to find a babysitter, and Matt suggested the two little boys would be all right with Jack.

"After all, he's sixteen," he said. "And the boys sleep like logs. We can put them to bed and leave the phone number of the restaurant."

Jack only shrugged when they asked him. "Of course, I'll be fine," he said.

Aldith looked at his broadening shoulders, at the dark hair he was wearing longer these days, and a shiver went through her. Jack's shrug reminded her so vividly of his father – it was uncanny, all the small shared gestures. She was noticing it more and more as Jack matured, and was pierced by a spike of anger that Victor had never asked for contact with his son. He had shaken his head when she'd told him she was pregnant, bewildered, as if he had wondered how such a thing could have occurred. He hadn't been unkind, just uninterested in fatherhood; even if he had proposed, Aldith wouldn't have wanted to marry him. She had told Jack that his father travelled abroad a lot, that he wasn't the type to settle with a family. Jack had seemed to accept Victor's absence, but perhaps secretly he felt abandoned. She worried that a day would come when Jack would want to meet his father and feared it could only result in disappointment.

Matt went to get the car out. It was raining lightly. Aldith looked around the tidy cottage, at Jack sprawled on the sofa in front of the television. She had already checked that Charlie and Aaron were asleep.

"See you when we get back," she said. "We won't be late. Ring if there's any trouble."

As Aldith closed the French doors, Jack flicked her a casual wave.

The police came to the restaurant, one male and one female officer. As soon as Aldith saw them her stomach flipped: she knew they had come to find her and Matt. She tugged at Matt's sleeve – he and Simon were deep in conversation; Julia had gone to the loo. The dining room buzzed with people eating expensive food and sipping expensive wines. In the soft light shed by silk-fringed lamps, the uniformed police hovered at the end of the bar like a pair of huge dark birds. Even before the waiter swivelled on his heel and pointed out their table, Aldith's hands had begun to tremble.

Jack had taken the keys to Aldith's car. She had not thought she needed to hide them from him. He had driven up their lane to the main road and flattened the accelerator on the long straight stretch towards the town. At the first bend, he'd braked too hard on the wet road. The policeman, a middle-aged man, shook his head, his face creased with sorrow. The car had jumped a ditch and hit a dry-stone wall. Death, the policeman said, must have been instantaneous. Later, Aldith would ask how the police had known they were at the restaurant, and they would explain that they'd traced her car registration to the cottage; they had found it unlocked, with the telephone number she had left for Jack beside the phone in the kitchen. The two little boys had been asleep and a policewoman had been called to sit with them.

They drove to the place where Aldith's elderly Morris lay crushed against a broken wall. Jack's body had been removed by ambulance. In their car headlights Aldith could see the shattered windscreen, the concertinaed bonnet, the glint of fragments scattered over the grass and among stones. She, too, felt crushed, barely able to breathe.

Aldith heard her mother laughing. "He'll be the death of us, that boy!" Neither she nor her mother would ever laugh again. There were needles of pain in her throat and behind her eyelids. At the cottage, Matt poured brandy; Julia and Simon came, and Julia wept and hugged them both.

"I'd stay with you," she said, "but there's Mollie."

Aldith dumbly shook her head. She was partially numb, and numb might be the best she could hope for.

She went every day to sit with Jack. They would ask her to wait for a few minutes in the pastel-coloured reception area while the man who was looking after her son made him ready for viewing in the chapel. The first time, she and Matt went together. They stood on either side of Jack and looked into the coffin at his waxen face. Covered by a starched white robe, there were no signs of injury, and Aldith wanted to ask how that was possible.

## Kandahar

After only a few minutes, Matt was anxious to leave.

"We can't do any good," he said. "We have to say goodbye."

But Aldith shook her head. "You go," she said. "I'll sit with him a while."

Alone, Aldith studied the beloved face, which she now saw was so different to Jack's living face that he could almost be someone else – a boy unknown to her. It was to do with the mouth, a narrowing that sketched meanness, or resentment for a lifetime of emotions destined to be withheld, frozen within a closed-lip smile. To subdue her panic, Aldith lowered her eyelids, and with an effort was able to impose upon the unfamiliar features a memory of Jack's expression as he had smiled at her from hundreds of photographs, from the kitchen doorway, from the living-room sofa. The strangeness was an illusion of death, or it was wrought by the funeral people who had not known her son. Lightly, she touched his hair and was comforted by its familiar softness.

Every afternoon she arrived and stayed until the office closed. Once, Julia came with her, but like Matt she became twitchy at the sight of the coffin and was soon anxious to leave. It was easier when she went alone. At each visit Aldith stroked Jack's icy cheek; she traced the faint shadow of his moustache. His skin, once merely pale, was now drained white, translucent, as unyielding under her fingers as porcelain; she could see the blue veins threaded beneath the surface.

A chair was brought for her, and Aldith sat beside Jack and talked. She told him about herself, about his father, and how he had come to be born. It hadn't been a loveless union, more like an adventure. She'd been in love with the romance of Victor Maddingly's life, with the glamour of the places he travelled to and returned from. Often he would bring her a souvenir. What had happened to that rug he'd given her? She could not remember. Or the mosaic boxes he'd bought for her in Fez? She had nothing left of that time, only this boy, and she would never again look into his green-gold eyes. Aldith ran a fingertip over the cold curve of Jack's forehead. He was at the height of his youthful beauty and would remain so in her memory.

As they waited for the coroner to release Jack for burial, Matt urged Aldith to give up her daily vigil. It was a form of self-torture that was only adding to her grief. He was coaxing at first, then insistent, and when Aldith declined to abandon her visits, Matt became offended, even resentful. She told Julia of his disapproval and saw in her friend's face, in its utter bewilderment, that she and Simon agreed – they all thought her need to sit with Jack's body was obsessive, excessive, and unhealthy. Only her mother understood.

"You go, if you want to," she said. "After all, it's your last chance."

Her final visit was on the morning of the funeral. It was chilly in the chapel, and there was an odour of antiseptic beneath the cloying scent of lilies. When she kissed her son's forehead, a light that had burned in Aldith since he was born was extinguished; she pressed the back of her hand to his cheek and finally registered his remoteness. Jack had gone to a distant land and he would not return, no matter how hard she willed it. She could hardly bear to leave, but in the end the man who was looking after Jack came in and whispered that it was time to get him ready for the funeral.

The church was full – there were teachers and students from Jack's new school, and people from the choir, and from Matt's work. Aldith recognised neighbours she had spoken to, the woman from the farm shop where she bought vegetables. Julia and Simon joined them in the front pew, with Mollie sitting quietly beside Charlie and Aaron.

The fatal blow to Matt and Aldith's marriage occurred on that first visit to the funeral home. Aldith couldn't understand Matt's withdrawal, his recoiling from Jack, and later his resentment. She thought of how Jack had become difficult since they'd moved from London. Children always knew more than adults suspected: perhaps he had sensed in Matt a preference for his biological sons. To Aldith, Jack's dying on the anniversary of her marriage was like a sign, and once this thought had lodged in her mind, their relationship soured. When Julia and Simon invited them for supper there was a new awkwardness between the four. The Ledwidges ate less and drank more; there were sudden, loaded silences.

"How are you two travelling?" Julia said, when she and Aldith were alone.

"Why do you ask?"

"You seem ... sort of strained together."

"Is it any wonder, after what happened?"

Julia took her hand. "I've always thought grief would draw a couple close."

"Jack wasn't Matt's child," Aldith said. "He doesn't feel the loss as I do."

Julia regarded her sorrowfully, but to Aldith's relief she did not talk about the stages of grief, or try to jolly her along.

Aldith went to stay with her mother. It was easier there, because the two of them were united in their loss; Aldith didn't have to pretend. Dora held her while she wept. They reminisced about the baby they had doted on, his fearlessness from a toddler, his adventurous spirit. Aldith knew that some of that came from Victor Maddingly.

She had written to Victor, telling him of Jack's death, and he'd telephoned to say how sorry he was to hear her news. Even though he and Jack had never met, Aldith could tell that Victor was shocked, and she'd wondered whether he regretted not having made an effort to be part of their lives.

Aldith brought the two little boys to Maida Vale. Julia rang every week to remind her of the life she'd abandoned – the cottage garden she had planted, the henhouse that awaited hens. But none of it held Aldith's interest now, and after a while Julia stopped calling. When Matt came to London at weekends to see the boys, he didn't stay with Aldith and Dora, but with friends who lived in his old digs.

That winter there was news of Aunt Ida's death, along with the surprise that she had bequeathed her house and its contents to Aldith. One dark December day, Aldith left the boys with her mother and drove to Hastings to collect the house keys from her aunt's solicitor. She let herself in by the back door. The yellow kitchen was shabbier than when she had last seen it, but the scrubbed pine table still stood in the centre of the room. She saw herself sitting with a blue and white teacup in her hand, a girl with a pony tail, while her aunt said that she was only young once and that she should spread her wings. What would have happened, Aldith wondered, if she had never answered Victor's advertisement in the *Bexhill Observer*? What if instead she had returned to London and found a different job? She would have been spared this wrenching grief, but she would have forfeited the bliss.

The telephone was connected, and as Aldith dialled the numbers for Victor's office she wondered whether he still wore the turquoise scarf, the silver bracelet. The number rang and rang, but there was no answer. It was a working day, the middle of the week. She had to assume the import business had folded. Victor must be fifty or fifty-five by now. Perhaps he had tired of travelling to those distant, dangerous places. She could walk to his house and perhaps she would. Just for a quick look.

Ida's blue and white teacups were arranged on the kitchen dresser. Aldith took one, filled it with tap water, and drank. She would sell this house and buy a place for herself and the boys that would make it easy for Matt to share in their upbringing. She wanted Charlie and Aaron to have happy childhoods to look back on – their lives mustn't be blighted by Jack's death.

She locked the back door and set out to walk to the house where Victor Maddingly had lived, the house where Jack had been conceived in the Balinese bed. The wind flapped her skirt around her legs, and Aldith buttoned her coat. Seagulls coasted in the wintry sky, their cries melancholy and urgent. The streets were almost empty, the traffic thin, and as she walked she wondered whether the citadel of Old Kandahar had survived the war in that country. She wondered whether it still loomed, rose-coloured, out of the tawny desert, and hoped with all her heart that it did.

# THE TOWER

Dorelia's parents had opposed her plan to go to art school. Her mother insisted that girls who went in for such a thing were likely too fast for their own good, while her father refused to pay for something so outlandish and without job prospects. Friends of theirs who had daughters were sending them to business college and he was adamant Dorelia would go too. Dorelia had argued; she had asked her art teacher to write a letter pointing out that her best subject all through high school had been art, but it was no good. Then, as she was miserably preparing to begin bookkeeping and typing classes, news came that her godmother May Fleury had died and bequeathed her a decent sum. Ignoring her mother's tears and her father's threats, Dorelia had arranged an interview at East Sydney Technical College and passed the entrance examination.

As soon as she was offered a place, she moved into a scruffy flat off Bayswater Road with two other students. It was on the first floor of a cavernous building in which the conversion from private house to flats had created corridors that led to blank walls, rooms that opened inconveniently into other rooms, and a few small marooned spaces with no apparent purpose. The student who had obtained the lease, Elizabeth Bunting, had seen at once that the superfluous spaces could be made into small studios.

The first time Dorelia set eyes on Elizabeth she was barefoot, wearing a pair of paint-stained men's trousers, and standing on a chair to unhook dusty floral curtains from a window in the small square studio space she had claimed as her own.

"You must be the new girl," Elizabeth said, dropping the curtains to the floor. "What a bit of luck, this light!"

Elizabeth had a great quantity of dark hair, which she wore bundled on the nape of her neck, or else swinging down her back in a tapering braid. She was tall and willowy, and everything about her was narrow, from her waist to her long thin hands and feet, her pale, narrow face. Beside her, Dorelia appeared slight, almost child-like. Yet she would soon learn that she and Elizabeth shared the same fierce determination to succeed and to prove their parents wrong, especially their fathers.

Elizabeth was from Sydney's west, a suburb Dorelia had only vaguely heard of. She pictured it as a harsh, hot place, where people went to work in factories, a far cry from her own middle-class North Shore upbringing, where women stayed at home after marriage, where they arranged tennis parties and endless charitable fundraisers. Elizabeth's two brothers were on the production line at a biscuit factory; her father was a mechanic. Her mother worked as a seamstress in a shirt factory, while moonlighting at home making bridesmaids' dresses.

"Four or five outfits all exactly the same, but cut to fit their different shapes and sizes. Can you think of anything more tedious?" Elizabeth rolled her eyes. "Giggling Gerties, we call Mum's clients. You should be there when they arrive to be fitted!"

But Dorelia saw that she was secretly proud of her mother's skills and learned that her mother, Alma, had supported Elizabeth's art school dream, paying the fees out of her sewing money.

Their other flat mate was Patricia Chandler, whose winged eyeliner and upswept hair gave her a permanently astonished appearance. Patricia's boyfriend was a music student, and she spent so much time at his share house that Dorelia and Elizabeth frequently forgot she was living with them.

On their doughnut days, one or other of the women often marvelled that their long friendship had sprung from a handwritten advertisement pinned to a campus noticeboard. Together they had completed the introductory and intermediate stages and embarked on the four-year diploma. Then, in their final year, Bunty had won a six-month study exchange at an art school in Paris. At the end of it she planned to stay on for the northern summer, and Dorelia was to join her in France.

"But she'll be *seventy-five* in January," Hannah said, as if this fact of their mother's life might have escaped her sister's notice. "At her age people move into sheltered housing, or a retirement village. It's *insane*, buying a place that's not much smaller than Number 10."

"I know," Gwenyth sighed.

Hannah could hear a dog barking in the background; its sharp, persistent yap made her grind her teeth until she remembered how much it had cost to crown those molars and hastily relaxed her jaw.

"Have you bought a dog?" she said irritably.

Her sister's voice was muffled, as if she had put her hand over the phone to speak to someone. The dog yapped twice more and was silenced.

"It belongs to a friend," Gwenyth said. "It's a Yorkshire terrier."

"Right. Well, are you quite certain Mum's going ahead with this mad plan?"

"Absolutely! She's even set a moving date."

Hannah knew the date, but it hadn't fully sunk in. Within minutes of the call in which she had first learned that their mother had sold the family house, she had phoned Gwenyth from Wellington and urged her to hasten to Number 10.

Gwenyth had arrived at Dorelia's door, flushed and agitated.

"Mum, Hannah says …"

"It's true," Dorelia had interrupted her to say firmly. "I'm moving house, two weeks on Friday."

"Hannah, Mum appeared quite normal," Gwenyth said, the dog yapping again in the background.

"How can she be? To have sold our family home without consulting us?"

After her sister had hung up, Hannah chewed viciously at a thumbnail. Only an unhinging, most likely brought on by grief, could account for her mother's recklessness. Or maybe it was that dotty old friend egging her on. Laurence had always said Elizabeth Bunting was as mad as a March hare, embittered by barrenness, he insisted, and then by early widowhood. Hannah would laugh when he said it, but she thought her brother cruel: after all, it wasn't Elizabeth's fault that she was childless, or that the man she had lived with – who for years Hannah had assumed was her husband – had died unexpectedly and left her poorly off.

When they were children, their mother would take them to Bunty and Willard's basement flat in Bellevue Hill. It was a long bus ride across the harbour bridge, and then a second bus from Wynyard Station. To Hannah it had seemed a world away from their own comfortable square white house in Balgowlah. To make matters worse, she would often get motion sickness and arrive half fainting. The flats, formed from a grand old dwelling that had long been shabby, were cut into the side of a cliff. Going down flight after flight of steps to reach the entrance, Hannah had clung to her mother's hand, fearful of tumbling into the weed-choked ravine below.

Inside, the rooms had been painted a deep red, and a grey that reminded Hannah of the skin of a Queensland blue pumpkin. They had been crammed with paintings set scarcely a finger's width apart. Willard had taught life drawing at the art school where Elizabeth and Dorelia had trained together. Elizabeth was a full-time artist, and the walls of the flat were crowded with her work – still life studies that Hannah now knew to be exceptional, though at the time it had been the studies of naked women, or (even worse) of naked men, that had both interested her and left her queasy with embarrassment.

More rarely, Elizabeth had visited them. Her clothing always reeked of oil paint, of turpentine, and cigarette smoke, and there would be charcoal dust, or perhaps just grime, under her fingernails. Ever fastidious, Hannah had judged her rough and grubby, but what she resented most was that whenever the two women were together her mother would be subtly altered, until she seemed like someone Hannah didn't know. Then for days after the visit, Dorelia would be restless and moody. Laurence had once said it was because their mother had given up art and her friend had not, and that he wished Bunty would stay away.

There was something else about Elizabeth Bunting – it had disturbed Hannah then and disturbed her still – and that was her habit of slowly turning her head to look at you, her gaze so steady and piercing that you felt she could see straight through your skull into your thoughts.

Before she stowed her mobile phone, Hannah checked her email. She had opened it a dozen times that morning, and still the inbox held nothing from Simon since the week before she left Sydney. In that message he had been counting the days until she arrived in Wellington, or so he'd said. How could someone be counting the days and then lapse into silence?

Hannah caught herself grinding her teeth as she climbed out of her hire car into the windswept street. If she didn't find coffee within the next five minutes she would explode. In the distance, people were sitting at tables outside a café. Tears leaked from the corners of her eyes as she lowered her head and charged into the wind. A sudden stinging signalled her mascara had run, and she rubbed at it with her fingers, knowing she must look a mess.

In the washroom she mopped up with tissues and scooped cold water into her hands to splash her face. Her mother's dark blue eyes stared back at her from the mirror. She longed to lock herself in one of the cubicles for a good cry, but she had a meeting in an hour with the librarian at Special Collections.

On her second coffee, Hannah felt steadier. She resisted the impulse to check her email. Maybe there would be a note this evening at the B&B, for it was Simon who had given her the name of the place in Thorndon. The thought came then that she had his home telephone number, although they'd had an unspoken pact that she was never to ring it. It was an easy number to remember and Hannah knew it by heart. She imagined a woman's voice at the other end. *Hello? Who is this?* How stupid she had been to think life would stay on hold for her until she was ready. If there was no note this evening she would *have* to ring. If necessary, she could pretend to have the wrong number.

Hannah swallowed the last of her coffee, shuddering as her empty stomach recoiled from its bitterness. And now it looked like her mother was losing the plot, aided and abetted by that dried up old stick Elizabeth Bunting. Hannah suspected the two of them still sometimes smoked when they got together, and she thought of the last time she'd had a cigarette between her own lips. *Oh, Simon!*

She felt an ache then, a throb of sexual longing, and simultaneously remembered the red walls of Bunty's dining room, those naked figures flaunting themselves against pillows, or propped on an elbow, women with their breasts and pubic hair exposed, the men with their ridiculous penises curled on muscular thighs. They were the first naked men she had ever seen, thought Hannah, the first male genitalia. Good God, why was she even *thinking* of this now!

As for those two old women, they might have done life drawing and painting back when it was seen as daring, but the two of them put together could never have suffered as she was suffering, going out of her mind for the sight, the sound, the touch of a lover.

# AT SWAN'S HOTEL

"You can start next week, if you like."

Mariel nodded. She had found the advertisement for the summer job pinned to a noticeboard at Australia House. The woman interviewing her, Grace Bell, was presently emptying a wardrobe in a small flat in St John's Wood, pressing tweed skirts, jackets, and silk blouses, into cardboard boxes stamped with the name of a firm of removalists. The flat was on the third floor of a lovely old building with windows that looked out over a leafy square. Currently in disarray, it belonged to Grace Bell's mother.

"Unfortunately, Mummy is an awful alcoholic," Grace said. "We've packed her off to rehab."

It wasn't the first time, Mariel gathered, and Grace was gloomy about the prospect of her mother's recovery.

"This was the worst," she said, explaining as she folded knitwear that her mother had persuaded a taxi driver to take her from London to Edinburgh, staying overnight at various hotels, in a week-long bender. "In North Yorkshire, Mummy was so out of it that the driver had to call an ambulance."

Mariel looked around at the walls papered in a soft pink stripe, at the lamps with silk shades; it was difficult to imagine someone – an elderly woman – afflicted by alcohol in such a setting. She watched Grace seal a carton with wide grey tape; she was a woman in her thirties, with a boyish figure and smooth fair hair. Her hands as they folded and packed clothing were quick and graceful; half-moons of shadow lay beneath her dark blue eyes.

"All the carpets have been ruined by spilled drink." Grace screwed up her face in distaste. "Particularly in the bedroom – can you smell it? There's someone coming to replace them tomorrow and afterwards the flat will be put up for sale."

"Can I help with anything?"

"Thanks, but I'm nearly done." Grace scribbled instructions for the train on the back of a drink coaster advertising Gordon's gin. "I'll see you next week, then."

The hotel Grace Bell ran with her husband Gerald was in East Sussex, on the edge of the ancient town of Rye. Painted white, with black trim on its eaves and window frames and its brass-knockered front door, it stood out cleanly against the grey stone buildings of the town and against the cloud-streaked sky. *Swan's Hotel* was lettered on the window-glass in black and a bright gold-leaf, and on a board above the double front doors a sleek white swan with a tiny golden crown on its head floated on a blistered swirl of cobalt paint.

In its entrance hall was the reception desk where Mariel was to greet guests and manage bookings. On the afternoon of her arrival a fire burned in the fireplace, and there were fresh flowers on the mantlepiece, as well as on a round table among copies of *Gardens Illustrated* and *The Lady*. Grace led her through the guests' lounge, a soothing room in which small brown birds perched among trellis and brambles on a faded, honey-coloured wallpaper. Dusky velvet curtains, elaborately swagged and fringed, were looped back and held by bird-shaped brass clasps.

Beyond the windows lay a cobbled courtyard dotted with potted topiary, some trimmed into the shapes of swans. A grandfather clock in the hall chimed the hour as Mariel followed Grace Bell up a narrow staircase. Years ago, when the hotel had been a private residence, Grace explained, this back stair had been used by servants. It led to the attics, which were for live-in staff, and it was in one of these small bright rooms that Mariel unpacked her belongings.

Her window overlooked the hotel's rear garden, which bordered the narrow thread of the River Rother. She could see a pair of swans, and there were ducks asleep on the hotel's lawn. On the river's far bank rose the grey patchwork of shapes that was the town. The room was simply furnished, with space to set up an easel; its diffused light would be perfect if the job ever allowed her time to paint. As she hung her few clothes in the wardrobe and tidied her hair before its mirror, Mariel felt as if she had accidentally dropped into a fairy tale. Of course, she was no princess, but here, she sensed, she would become a different girl to the one who had left Australia, different even to the girl who in London had stood for hours before the paintings of John Singer Sergeant, of Monet, and Whistler.

On a sheet of the hotel's notepaper, she drew a map of the town showing Swan's Hotel, with its regal little signature bird, its topiary pots, and its garden with three silver birch trees and white-painted iron furniture. She slipped it between the pages of a letter she was writing to her sister Frieda, and then, gazing across the river towards the town, she tried to summon the rough red landscape of far western New South Wales where she had been born and raised and where Frieda and their two brothers still lived.

From Rye, it was almost impossible to believe in that town's existence, though her bag contained letters from home, some with photographs. The latest of these showed Frieda in her bare front yard holding up her newborn baby boy, Jesse. Beside her, the older child Sheena leaned towards the camera with a disconcertingly naked gaze. Frieda's husband Ryan must have taken the picture. Mariel couldn't visualise Ryan, or her sister and their children, in this muted landscape; it was difficult to reconcile the dual realities of England and Australia.

Until she got the hang of her reception duties, juggling bookings was stressful. Guests constantly surprised her with their demands: a pot of lemon and ginger tea must be made with chunks of fresh ginger and plenty of lemon; a hot water bottle was to be inserted into a bed one hour before a certain guest retired; a postage stamp of the correct value to convey a letter by air to Iceland was urgently required. And their questions were so repetitive: Were there really no late-night bars in the town? Where was the nearest Indian takeaway? What time was the next train to London? She considered typing up a sheet of answers.

But the hotel itself was a revelation, for every room had its particular beauty. Aside from the little birds on the honey-coloured paper in the lounge, there was a scarlet dining-room with French doors that opened onto the garden, and through which wafted the scent of new-mown grass, and the salty, musty, not-unpleasant odour of the river. Clocks chimed charmingly on the hour and the half-hour, and the books and oil paintings, watercolours, and etchings, that had been missing from every house Mariel had ever lived in were plentiful. Seeing such things in an art gallery, a bookshop, or a museum, was one thing, it was to be expected, but to wake to them every day, to look up from some mundane task and find oneself in their midst was, for Mariel, a kind of ecstasy.

The hotel had its history, too. Grace showed her a door frame in the kitchen with notches in the wood where small children had stood to have their heights measured.

"These date back to when Swan's was the home of Gerald's great uncle, Edwin Bell. He had four sons, and his wife Alicia died giving birth to their youngest."

Grace pointed to the scratched initials: *CB, AB, PB, HB.* "The boys were raised by Edwin's housekeeper, a Mrs Reynolds. I'm guessing it was she who measured them, since the marks were made here in her domain."

"When did the house become a hotel?"

"Well, all four boys were killed in the First World War and their father never really recovered from their loss. After he died, the house was left to Gerald's aunt, Eviane Bell, who ran it as a guest house."

"And that was when it got its name?"

"Yes, Eviane found the old pub sign with the swan in an antique shop and had it hung over the front door. We have some guests who return every year because their parents brought them as children, and one or two who come because their parents came when *they* were children!"

In some strange way Mariel felt defeated by this story, for nothing at home could match its continuity. The houses she had lived in had all been built within the memory of the people who lived in them and none had much history.

Of the paintings that crammed the hotel's walls, there were two she had fallen in love with. The first was a portrait of a woman with a mass of dark wavy hair and a face like one of Rosetti's pre-Raphaelite models. The woman wore a severe black jacket over a white, full-skirted dress; she stood with eyes cast down against an ochre wall on which the shapes of small birds flitted among brambles. It was the restrained colour scheme that first drew Mariel's eye: the painting's carefully modulated greys and telling use of black were reminiscent of James MacNeill Whistler. The warm ochre background spilled into the shadows, where the woman's right hand lightly rested on the sleek black head of a whippet. In the bottom right-hand corner was a small flowing signature: *E. Bunting*.

"The woman in that picture is Eviane Bell," Grace told her. "It was painted by a young Australian who stayed here one winter, and it was almost certainly offered as payment for her bed and board."

Grace explained that in the off-season Eviane had taken in artists and writers and charged them a pittance, or sometimes she had just accepted a few drawings, or a painting, in exchange for a room.

"God knows how the writers paid. I think she was always hoping that one of her guests would become famous and she could cash in whatever they'd given her and retire."

The other piece Mariel loved showed a young woman in a green dressing-gown sitting in a black rattan chair; she wore her hair loose and clasped a book in one long, elegant hand. The room she sat in was sparsely furnished, and its polished floorboards flowed like dark water under her beautiful bare white feet. The view through the window behind her was the view of the town from Mariel's bedroom, and the artist had used chalk-pale colours, so that the figure appeared to be fading into the room, the room fading from the canvas. A little brass plate set into the deep wooden frame gave the picture's title: *The Convalescent*. It was perfect, and each time she saw it Mariel was gripped with a longing to paint something half as fine.

"Painted by another of Eviane's winter lodgers," Grace said, when she came upon her admiring it.

Lying in bed at night with the river scent drifting through her window, Mariel imagined the conversations there must have been in the scarlet dining-room at mealtimes during those long-ago off-seasons. She wished she could have been a part of it. Meanwhile, she greeted guests and attended to their requests with a smile. In her precious free hours she worked at her easel, perfecting her greys in views of the town in every kind of weather, or setting up still life studies with objects borrowed from Grace's kitchen, or picked up in the town's bric-a-brac shops.

Rye's night life revolved around its many pubs, and in Mariel's first weeks Grace and Gerald took her out and introduced her around until she knew enough people to have a drink with. As an Australian, she was a bit of a novelty, and only had to appear in the doorway of a pub for someone to wave her over to join them.

It was on one of those nights in The Ship Inn that Grace Bell introduced Mariel to Nick McCloud. The English summer had not been particularly good but there was a sun-washed look about Nick, as if his skin had trapped some hidden warmth. He could almost be Australian. Mariel found herself answering his questions about snakes. Everyone in England seemed obsessed with the fact of Australia's snakes, and she was often torn between downplaying their presence and offering wild exaggerations of family stories.

"We kept long pieces of fencing wire handy in the house when I was a kid," she said. "You can kill a snake with a length of wire, although it's said they never completely die until the sun goes down."

Mariel was gratified by the cries of horror this drew from Grace and Gerald and by the intensity of Nick McCloud's gaze.

"Surely that's a myth, the sun part?" Nick said.

Mariel shook her head. "My grandfather believed snakes take their heat from the sun. It's not something I'd put to the test."

She and Nick ran across each other most Friday nights at The Ship, or The Standard, and after a few evenings spent in each other's company Nick offered to pick her up in his car and drive out of town for a pub meal. This soon became a regular date, and inevitably, after one of these outings, Nick brought her back to his place for a late-night drink. The house he lived in was one half of a two-storey, square, brick box; its windows looked out over a shingle beach and the sea. There was the curve of a bay with a lighthouse set on its ancient headland. It was a warm evening, and when Nick opened sliding glass doors, a sea breeze billowed the long net curtains.

They listened to music lying in Nick's bed, and Mariel found herself thinking it would be a struggle to get up and return to the hotel.

"Why do you have to leave, anyway?" Nick said.

"I have to be at work first thing."

"So, we'll set the alarm, and I'll drive you in early."

Soon they were meeting in every free moment. Between her job, and Nick, there was little time to paint. At work, passing through the small breakfast room where Grace and Gerald took their meals, *The Convalescent* was a constant reproach.

By now Mariel was spending every evening with Nick, but when she wrote to her sister she avoided mentioning his name. This puzzled her so much that she wrote a letter in which she told Freddie she'd met someone and that they were in love, but before she put the stamp on, she tore it up and threw it away.

A local gallery hung some of her views of the town and sold a few to the tourists. But by then the season was over and with it her summer job at Swan's Hotel. Mariel moved in with Nick and looked for other work.

In her lunch break at a dull office job, she wrote to Frieda of her love, and this time she posted it. She and Nick were solid, and before long they left the square ugly house for a house with a garden, the first of their marriage. There would be time to pursue her painting once they were settled, Nick said, and Mariel believed this too. But the old brick house with its curving roofline filled an emptiness that had gnawed at her since school days. Waking to light streaming through its diamond-pane windows, watching the bare, sprawling limbs of apple and pear trees slowly fill with blossom and leaf, and then with fruit, Mariel could not believe her luck. She was like a hermit crab that had at last stumbled upon the perfect shell.

There was always so much to be done in the garden. The house, too, was only at its best when filled with jars of preserves, when scented with furniture polish, or the yeasty smell of home-made bread. Mariel hand-sewed curtains and roamed far and wide in search of antique and second-hand pieces for their rooms. Almost without her noticing, the craving to create something fine with her paintbrush that had brought her to London, to stand in the National Gallery and the Tate with tears in her eyes, gradually lost its urgency.

# THE TOWER

Gwenyth hovered in the doorway, her face so pale that Dorelia was flooded with remorse at having caused her distress.

"I've just made coffee," she said, gently taking her daughter's hand and drawing her inside.

"But Mum, why on earth didn't you say anything? How could you do something so, well, *major*, without asking us?"

Dorelia smiled, hearing Hannah's inflection in Gwenyth's reproach. But asking permission? Her remorse lost its edge. The king was dead, but she was still queen. And queens had sovereignty. If she were a different sort of queen-woman she might have screamed: *Off with their heads!*

Gwenyth cast a tearful gaze around the living room, and Dorelia saw that she was dreading the tongue-lashing she would receive from Hannah, and perhaps from Laurence, for having allowed this to happen on her watch.

"What will you do with everything?" Gwenyth said. "These things we've grown up with."

They stood close, staring at the familiar pattern of the worn Turkish rug and at all the cherished belongings that, for the moment, still occupied their usual places. Dorelia saw that these things gave Gwenyth, and probably Hannah and Laurence, the impression that the life on which their own lives had been built was – although thoroughly shaken – still intact. They did not notice, or if they did they had never said anything, that the table lamps with their red silk shades shed a colder light since Geordie's death, that all the singing colours of the room – of the pictures and even the rich old rug – had sunk an octave. Could they really not see that despite her polishing, the lacquer-ware box in which their father had once kept his cigars had lost its lustre? And was she to spend what remained of her life as museum keeper, preserving clocks and paintings and assorted bric-a-brac, lavishing energy on silver that was never used, dusting mahogany chairs and tables in anticipation of Christmas and the occasional Sunday lunch? Once these objects were dispersed to new homes, all that they had held together for so long would be irrevocably altered, as she had been altered – scarred, even – by the battles of parenting. There had been Laurence's decade-long anguish over his acne, and Hannah's hangover years to be weathered; Gwenyth's teenage eating disorder had almost finished them both. No, she had given these children life, nurtured them from helpless babes to functional adults – surely whatever time she had left should be her own.

"Take anything you want," she said, sliding a consoling arm around her daughter's waist. "I've put green stickers on the things I'll keep. Everything superfluous can go to the auction rooms."

She was moving very little of her old life to the tower, just a few cherished belongings and a ruthlessly reduced collection of books.

On the morning after Gwenyth's visit, Dorelia received a call from her GP's receptionist asking her to attend the clinic and offering an appointment on the following afternoon. Her doctor wanted to check in with her and review her medications, the receptionist said. When Dorelia pressed for more information, the woman's voice became vague.

Her GP, Ted Canning, had also been Geordie's doctor; they had known him for more than twenty years. Dorelia was suddenly grateful for this long-standing relationship, when she realised from Ted's blustering embarrassment that one or more of her children had attempted to convince him she was incompetent.

"I suppose it was Hannah," Dorelia said sadly.

Ted Canning wriggled in his swivel chair. "Actually, it was Laurence, but Hannah rang and spoke to my receptionist." He studied Dorelia, his gaze non-judgemental. "So, what's all the fuss about? What's got them hopping?"

How could they have called her doctor! It was humiliating. Dorelia looked Ted in the eye while she spoke. "I've sold the house," she said, "and bought another one. Apparently, they think I shouldn't have done it on my own."

"It's not that long since you lost Geordie," Ted said, leaning back in his chair. "Any problems with sleep? Loss of appetite?"

"About the same as always for the sleep," she said. "A bad night, occasionally, but mostly it's all right. I've never taken sleeping pills, as you know. And I do still get hungry, just not for such quantities of food as the children think I should be eating."

Ted took her blood pressure and blood sugar; he pressed his stethoscope against her heart.

"All seems to be in working order," he said.

"Aren't you going to ask me to name the prime minister of Australia?" said Dorelia.

Ted shook his head and answered gruffly, "I see no call for daft questions."

The packing required all her stamina. After overseeing the removal of furniture, both to her children's homes and to the auction house, Dorelia fell exhausted into bed each day at dusk. Her bed, hers and Geordie's, was to go to the tower house, so at least she had that up until the last moment. Bunty helped her sort and wrap the china. Dorelia would keep what was left of the dinner service she and Geordie had started married life with; she would keep the mismatched blue and white tea set and the spongeware serving dishes. Not that she would cook and serve large meals in the tower house, but the sight of their hand-sponged patterns had always cheered her whenever she opened a cupboard.

Together she and Bunty extracted a basic set of kitchen tools and equipment from the accumulated ironmongery. Hannah had claimed the Royal Worcester and the sideboard in the dining room. Laurence was to have the dining table with the twelve balloon-back chairs and Geordie's decanters, while his daughter Penelope, a music student, was to inherit her grandfather's piano. Gwenyth had come, trailing her new love, a sturdy girl with delicate tattoos and a messy bun of strawberry blonde hair; she'd asked for the watercolours from the hall and the green velvet chaise. Dorelia hugged and kissed both her daughter and her lover, Mel, and found a roll of bubble wrap for the pictures.

It was beyond exhausting, but at last it ground to a close. And there she was, in the sparsely furnished living room of the tower house, pouring bubbles for herself and Bunty.

Bunty raised her glass and touched it gently against Dorelia's.

"Here's to sovereignty," Dorelia said.

Bunty smiled. "And subversion."

The tower house gathered Dorelia in as if it had been waiting for her. Crossing the threshold under the pale plaster eyes of the little watch-woman she felt protected, unlike in the old house, where at night the dark, empty bedrooms had made her feel like a piece of flotsam washed up on a deserted shore. Garnet and green stained-glass panels on either side of the front door threw down dazzling lozenges of coloured light in the little entrance hall. The tower house exuded such a companionable warmth, it was as if someone she'd been sharing a joke with had just slipped into the next room to fetch something, leaving a trail of laughter.

On the hall table she set an old pewter jug filled with the white narcissi that were popping up everywhere in the garden. The black and white tiled floor, with her red umbrella leaning in a corner, the purity of the flowers in the jug – their pale edges blurring in her peripheral vision – was so pleasing, that she could stand in the hall and gaze at it for minutes at a time. The ground floor rooms had accepted the few belongings she brought to them with ease, and the weight of all she had not brought filled Dorelia with an almost holy relief. A lifetime's clutter had become other people's responsibility; she no longer had to dust, to polish, to be reminded by a particular presence, of things that had become painful. Austerity was a remembered pleasure, one her daughters could not fathom.

"Isn't it a bit grim?" Gwenyth said. "Have you got more stuff in the shed, or somewhere?"

"I have everything I need," Dorelia said firmly. She hated letting them into the tower room, but of course they all insisted on trooping up to look – Gwenyth and Mel, Hannah, back sooner than she had planned from Wellington, with her long-suffering partner Geoff and their two silent teenage boys. Hannah had given Laurence a virtual tour on her phone. Dorelia bore it all with a smile, knowing that if their opinions were negative it didn't matter: the house was hers, and at least for now there was nothing they could do about it.

When they had gone, she was at last able to arrange her workspace. The removal men – cursing the narrowness of the stairwell – had unrolled the Persian rug from Geordie's study to warm the floorboards and had installed her wing chair and its matching ottoman. There was a bookcase, and an adjustable reading lamp on a side table. Extra books, and there were always extras, were stacked in neat piles around the edges of the room where she would not trip over them.

Climbing the stairs in the mornings was an exquisite pleasure, and where once the days had seemed interminable, they now sped by as if winged. In the mornings she forged ahead with her writing, and after a sandwich at midday she often napped in her chair. In the afternoons she would read over what she had written earlier, or rest with a book. The loveliest hour of all was dusk, when she would turn off the lights and watch for the first appearance of the evening star. It was Geordie she thought of then, and in the dimming light she often sensed his presence.

When the last light faded from the windows, Dorelia made her way down to prepare a simple supper, which she ate at the kitchen table listening to the radio. After washing up, she would read in bed until she fell asleep. This was the pattern of her days, with Thursday mornings reserved for a doughnut run to the good bakery with Bunty. On Sundays the two of them would drive out somewhere for a pub lunch.

Rapunzel's witch was proving tricky to redeem. There was the blinding of the prince, and the casting out of Rapunzel, which Dorelia felt was an act of gratuitous cruelty.

Bunty argued for the witch. "She suffers the pain of betrayal," she said. "Rapunzel has deceived her. I hear that's not uncommon in teenage girls."

"Yes, but we don't usually punish them for it by casting them into the desert."

Bunty said, "Girls in our day, girls who got pregnant, the Catholic ones especially, were sent away so that no one would know. Because if word got out, the stigma was life-long. What was that if not being cast into the desert?"

They sat silently together for a long time after that, each of them vividly immersed in the past, but unwilling to bring it into the room where they had been laughing and eating doughnuts.

Finally, with a tentative glance at Bunty, Dorelia said, "So the witch was a victim of her own upbringing. Perhaps she herself was the offspring of a girl like Rapunzel."

"I think you're on the right track there," Bunty said.

Afterwards, Dorelia plunged ahead with her work until she thought she could show that the witch was as much a prisoner of social pressure as Rapunzel was a prisoner in the tower. She was moved by Rapunzel's loneliness, as, perhaps, was the witch, for her last gift to the girl she'd wanted as a daughter was the spell that made a healing potion of her tears. The witch must have foreseen that Rapunzel would reunite with the blind prince, and when she did she would have the power to restore his sight. In the end the two young people would live happily ever after, while the witch would lose all she had held dear. The brothers Grimm had made her disappear, but in Dorelia's story she would retreat to her tower, pulling herself up into it by dint of her enormous will. There, released from all influences, including the longing for a child that society had primed her with, she would study the stars and work up spells to do good in the world.

"She mightn't go as far as good works," said Bunty.

"No," Dorelia agreed, "I've probably taken it a bit too far."

"I don't see why," Bunty said severely, "you don't just allow her to be creative."

# LIFE SUPPORT

Rifle-crack; bird flap: some mad bugger with a gun. Jesse peers into the bush on the far side of the clearing where the dawn landscape looks stonewashed, but no one runs towards him waving a shotgun. It is his second morning in the car, the first alone. Ozzie had gone late yesterday, trudging towards the highway to hitch to town. He'll have said he slept at a mate's house, that no one woke him for school. Ozzie's old man will've given him a spray. Ozzie had wanted Jesse to go with him.

"What's the point in staying out here?"

But it wasn't Ozzie's mother's car they'd slid out of the driveway in the early hours, creeping along Knox Street without headlights and then roaring away up the racecourse road, eventually running aground on the edge of the scrub.

She'll be waking soon, his ma, Freddie. Jesse pictures her curled in the middle of her big rumpled bed, Benny snoring alongside and wedged between them the yellow blur of Twisties the cat. Across the hall, his sister Sheena will be out to it, her head on the pillow – gnawed-looking pink hair, with fierce dark roots.

"It's a thing!" she'd said, when he asked her why she liked it.

His ma never goes to the hairdresser, not since she read how swimming with dolphins had helped some kid like Benny. Any

## The Tower

spare cash goes into the dolphin fund. But that time they'd driven him to the beach, Benny had screamed his head off – at the waves foaming in scallops at their feet, at the seagulls squabbling over scraps. They had walked to the end of the jetty, and Freddie had held Benny up to face the mirror-ball glitter of the ocean. But Benny had screamed even louder then, and when eventually they'd soothed him with ice cream, he'd sat digging sand with his back to the water.

"Digging deep enough to get to China," Freddie had said, and she had laughed, but her eyes had welled up.

Jesse knows they'll never get Benny near the ocean and even if they do he'll be freaked out by dolphins. Swimming with them might do his ma good though. She's strung out most of the time. Jesse rubs at his sleep-crusted eyes. She'll be panicking because he's missing. He pictures her smoking, the nervy way she flicks at the lighter. She'll have smoked a lot last night. Smokes are the one thing she spends money on and he wishes she wouldn't. He hates seeing her hunched out on the back veranda, because since Benny was diagnosed Freddie has never smoked inside the house.

He's wrecked her car – well, the engine sounds terminal. When he saw the keys on the table, he should've resisted the impulse. He hears his teacher, Miss James, telling him it's time he started making better choices. Miss James. Emily. She's the nicest teacher he's had in twelve years of school. Once, when he'd arrived late because he'd had to walk Benny to day-care, and on the way there his little brother had darted into the road and nearly got run over, Miss James had noticed his hands shaking. After class she had kept him behind and he'd blurted out that he'd been frightened, and then angry with his brother for almost getting killed.

"What's the point of Benny," he'd said, "if he can never have a decent life?"

And he had really thought at that moment that it might have been better if the car hadn't swerved, if at the last moment the driver hadn't spotted the figure with a Crows guernsey jammed on over a grey hoodie, dashing on a collision course with his front bumper.

Miss James had sat beside him and spoken softly.

"Jesse," she said, "never forget that Benny, for all his difficulties, was made with a purpose."

He knew she meant God, and at that moment he had been willing to believe. If only Miss James was right and his brother's life would add up to something, or at least become manageable. His mum thinks the same. Not that God made Benny the way he is for a reason, but that he was born for her, to grow her patience, to make sure she will always have something to live for. Even so, she had struggled to keep going after Dad's accident. They'd all been gutted, but for her it was worse.

He and Sheena had been at school, and the principal had summoned Sheena to his office and said that she and her brother were to go straight home. Benny was just a toddler then and they already knew he had a major problem. It had really bothered their dad, and Sheena thought maybe it had even contributed to his accident. Jesse doesn't see how it could've. And it was weird, but Benny finally being diagnosed had kicked their mother into gear. From then on, she had dedicated herself to living for the longest time, because Benny will grow bigger but he will never grow up. Sheena will leave home as soon as she can, and Jesse knows that if anything happens to their mother it will be up to him to look out for Benny.

The chill falling from the windows sets him shivering. He reaches into the back for his spare hoodie, and that is when he sees the fox. She is standing between the car and the scrub. Thin sunlight kindles a blaze in her coat, and as the light intensifies, the fur flames. Jesse squints, as if protecting his eyes from her heat. He reaches for the door handle with the ridiculous intention of crossing the clearing – like she will wait tamely for him to stroke her fur. Before he can open the door the fox turns away towards the scrub, and the pristine white chest is streaked with blood. She is gone before he can unfold his sleep-cramped limbs out of the front seat – her exit, though marred by a limp, is graceful, a rufous blur.

When Jesse reaches the spot where she stood there are drops of blood on the grainy yellow soil. He squats to scrutinise a smudge in the dirt that might be a paw print, and then his eyes fill and his chest tightens and heaves. Jesse puts out a hand to steady himself until the jagged sobs subside. After a few minutes he stands and wipes his nose along his sleeve. What if someone saw him wussing. But there is no one to see, not even the wounded fox. Not even the mongrel who shot her.

The sun warms his back as he reaches into the car for his drink bottle. He will have to leave before he runs out of water. That is, if he intends going back. Jesse sips, careful not to swallow too much, although he wants to gulp it down. It is the first time he has admitted there might be an alternative to going home.

Jesse turns towards the tortured shapes of blackened branches and the explosion of new growth on what Ozzie reckons are peppermint gums. The fire that swept through here, summer before this one, is already half forgotten by the bush. The sun flares over the rim of the hill; thoughts come at him in a rush. He sips again from the bottle and shrugs. His phone is in the shallow recess between the front seats – he misses the feel of it in his hand, but it's low on power; if he turns it on there'll be missed calls and texts from his ma, and he doesn't know what to say. He still isn't sure.

Walking away from the car, Jesse squats to stare again at the blood. A lizard slithers into a bush; from further away comes the dry, protesting cry of a crow. A breeze stirs the new leaves of the peppermints, as Jesse follows the fox's trail.

Freddie Barry wakes and fumbles under the pillow for her phone. Benny lies on his back beside her, so still and silent that she scrambles her other hand free of the bedclothes to touch his cheek: his skin is warm and smooth and there is the faint movement of his breath. Reassured, she rolls away and stares at the phone, but there is no message from Jesse. She slides out of bed and hurries along the passage to his room, where everything is as he left it two nights ago. It smells of Lynx deodorant and another, fainter, boy-scent that reminds her of her brothers. The emptiness is a kick in the guts, and Freddie hugs herself as she stalks towards the kitchen.

The hum of the kettle is lonely this morning. She tries Jesse's number, but his phone is still off. Making coffee one-handed, she calls her brother.

"Don? He's still not back."

Her brother's voice is thick with sleep as he urges her to try Jesse's friends again.

"They'll know. Mates always know."

The sun on the back deck warms her arms, her cold hands, as she makes the calls and listens to the vague responses. No one has seen him. Nobody knows. Ozzie O'Donoghue sounds even more evasive than when she spoke to him last night.

"Ozzie, if you know where he is —"

"Don't worry, Mrs Barry. I'm sure Jesse is fine."

"Yeah, well, thanks," she says lamely, knowing she can't accuse the boy of lying.

Freddie brings up her brother-in-law's number on her phone and stares at it for a long moment, then swipes it away without calling. The coffee tastes bitter, and she flings the rest of it over the side of the deck and goes indoors. In the hall mirror, freckles stand out on her cheeks like someone has thrown tan paint at a canvas. Her hair needs a wash, but it will have to wait.

Jesse has taken her car, and if she reports it he will lose his learner's licence. Freddie stares through the kitchen window at the empty carport – maybe he ought to lose it, teach him a lesson. Benny will wake soon. Her stomach churns – she is already exhausted, and the day has barely begun. But its Benny's morning for the special needs place, so at least she has a breathing space.

Freddie takes cereal from the cupboard and finds Benny's Spiderman bowl. When she was Sheena's age, it was their mother who'd caused them grief; she remembers the toe-curling shame of having a mother people gossiped about. But every family has its dramas, and one of these days they will find a treatment for Benny. In the meantime, it would help if people could just accept him for who he is.

Ozzie hates lying to Mrs Barry, her of all people. She is always so kind, never minding if he hangs around all afternoon and half the night with Jesse because he hates going home. Two or three times a week she asks him to stay for tea. Even though anyone can see she has her hands full, she sets another place at the kitchen table like it is no bother. Ozzie tries to remember whether his own mother was like that, welcoming his friends as if they were family, but there is no picture in his mind. Probably he'd been too young to have friends over when she went away. It was a long time ago. His old man never asks anyone to eat with them. And fair enough, because he has to work, and the shopping and cooking are extra.

His father is banging around in the kitchen, and Ozzie wants to get his clothes on before he talks to him. He messages Jesse – *text your mum* – and wonders whether Jesse still has any charge on his phone; he wonders how much trouble there'll be about the car and about the maths test they've missed. He needs to get his clothes on because his teacher wants his father to come to school for a meeting, and Ozzie has to break it to the old man before he leaves for work.

Freddie calls a taxi to take her and Benny to his special needs class. When she leaves him there and steps out into the street, she begins to breathe for what feels like the first time that morning. Briefly, the weight of the house, with Jesse's empty bedroom, eases its pressure on her skull. Freddie dawdles along the wide, dusty footpath towards a sandwich board that announces coffee and homemade cakes. The Little Flower Cafe and Collectables is quiet this morning, as she pays for a flat white and a muffin and carries them to the corner furthest from the till. The customers, mainly mothers snatching ten minutes of peace, smile and nod, but they do not invite her to sit with them. Being widowed keeps them at a distance, and Freddie's lips curve in the glimmer of a smile – silver linings are to be found in even the darkest pocket.

She will never be certain whether Ryan's death was an accident, but it was her doing, no question. There was no traffic that morning on the racecourse road, just Ryan on his motorbike with his helmet unbuckled. He often wore it dangling loose, despite the message it gave the children. But you couldn't tell him it was stupid bravado he should have outgrown years ago. You couldn't tell Ryan anything, only she had told him things that morning that had got his attention.

"I'm pregnant," she'd said.

He'd put down his can of coke, grinning. "How long have you known?"

"About three weeks, but don't get excited because I want a termination."

"You can't be serious!"

He'd tried to put his arms around her, but she had held herself away from him, shoulders stiff.

"I've already talked to Doctor Walsh."

"Without telling me –"

"Ryan, I can't look after a baby, not with Benny."

At the mention of their son, Ryan's face had darkened. "It's not likely to happen twice, Freddie. They told us that. You heard them."

"I did. But I'm saying Benny is all I can manage."

"Come on, Freddie, you won't have to do it all on your own."

Resentment, bottled up over nights when he went out with mates while she stayed home with the children, rose in Freddie's throat. Mornings when he had promised to help out later and instead went to the pub, or the betting shop. He would promise help with a baby, but help would never come.

She had wanted to hurt him, to seize control.

"I'm not sure if it's yours," she'd said.

"You *what*?"

She shook her head. "I'm sorry, Ryan."

His hands were heavy on her shoulders; she felt the press of his thumbs at her throat.

"Well, who the fuck then?"

Freddie's legs had threatened to buckle. "It's yours. Of course it is. I was being flippant."

He'd stared darkly at her, assessing. She had managed not to look away.

"It was a bad joke," she said. "I'm sorry. But I meant it about the termination."

He might have hit her, but instead he slammed out the door, and she heard the Honda's roar.

His brother Jordan had come to break the news about the accident. They'd stood in the kitchen avoiding each other's eyes, the two of them shocked, guilty. Ryan was in intensive care, Jordan said. His helmet had come off in the crash and the doctor said there was brain damage.

"Did you … did he … " He'd looked at her for the first time, stricken.

Freddie shook her head. "I didn't tell him."

She had been going to tell, but with Ryan's hands on her she'd suddenly been scared witless. Three children they'd had together, and she'd realised in that moment that she didn't know what Ryan Barry might be capable of, not really.

At the hospital, her thoughts chaotic, she had told the doctor that they should switch off Ryan's life support because he wouldn't want to live with brain damage.

"He couldn't stand it," she said. "And we have a special needs child." All at once she was sobbing. "I can't look after another living soul."

The doctor had stared at her gravely. "Mrs Barry there is nothing to 'switch off' as you put it. Your husband's condition is critical, but for the moment he is supporting his own life."

Freddie sips her coffee. It tastes no better than the brew she made at home; she can't eat the muffin.

A neighbour had stayed with the children while she went for the procedure. There was no one else she could have asked. For the first time in years, she had longed for her sister, but Mazz was overseas. Ryan's parents never knew she'd been pregnant, and she hadn't even considered telling Jordan. It was over quickly, and a week later she was at Ryan's bedside when he died, though God only knew if he had wanted her there.

Freddie has started writing a letter to her sister. The writing pad is in her handbag, and she pulls it out and looks over the start she's made.

> *Dear Mazz, I was clearing out a cupboard the other day and found that old scrapbook you filled with drawings. If you ever wanted to see it, I could put it in the post. The drawings are so good and you were only a kid at the time. Sheena's got the same creative streak, and I'm waiting to see what she wants to do with it. Both of you got it from Mum, I reckon, because Dad never had an arty bone in his body ...*

She stops reading and fumbles for a pen. She could finish this and post it on the way home. But with the pen in her hand, she can't think of anything more to write.

"Oh, Jesse, please come home!" She has whispered this aloud, but when she looks around the cafe, it appears no one has heard.

## The Tower

The path is uphill, over red, powdery soil. It's tough on Jesse's calves. He should be fitter, and he'll suffer when footy training starts – if he goes back home. The fox is losing more blood; there are continuous dribbles now rather than drops and splashes.

He'll run out of water. How long would it take to die, he wonders? How painful would it be? His mother would be broken up about it, but it'd be one less of them for her to worry about. Jesse knows he'll never be as selfless as his mother. One day Benny will be man-sized, and when Jesse thinks of a future in which he'll be responsible for his brother, his chest feels like it's filled with rocks. If Benny was made with a purpose, it means that he was, too. And Jesse wants a different life, a life on his own terms.

The fox is stretched out in thin shade, pink tongue hanging from her open mouth. She's dead, and her fur is dulled; her white front is soaked with blood. Jesse squats and runs a hand over her. Her body is warm, both from the sun and from the life that has only recently departed. He looks around for something to cover her with, but there is nothing. And then he sees that she's been feeding young.

He pushes on up the last few yards, to an opening between two boulders. There in a shallow burrow are her two pups, tiny creatures with blunt, questing noses. When he scoops them up, they squirm in his hands, hearts palpitating against his palms. They'll die without their mother. Death by starvation and dehydration. Jesse looks around for some clue to saving them, but there is only silence, and the sun climbing higher. He'll have to put them out of it. Jesse's never killed anything, but he thinks he can manage. One quick knock for each pup – they'll hardly know what's hit them.

He settles them on some leaves and finds a rock, weighs the heft of it in his hand. But the pups start squirming towards him as if they want to be picked up. He gazes at them – tiny, helpless – and knows he can't dash their brains out. The fox's body is still warm. Maybe the young can feed, a last drink to tide them over.

It's gross, feeding from a carcass, but Jesse has no better plan. He carries the cubs to the fox, and they latch on. Watching them suckle, he thinks of his mother the night before he left, white-faced with exhaustion, mashing potatoes while Benny smashed a wooden spoon against the saucepan cupboard. Jesse takes a careful sip from his flask.

When the cubs drop off, he nestles them in the front pockets of his hoodie, and his throat thickens with grief. What's the point of foxes, he wonders? There is a heaviness in his head like he sometimes gets when he goes to Ozzie's house, the two of them on their phones, camped in a wilderness of unwashed clothes and dishes, while Ozzie's old man sits in front of the television, watching sport and drinking. It's the mess of all their lives that disturbs him, though he has no clue what can be done about it.

In his pockets the cubs are asleep, their paws twitching now and then against his belly. Probably they are dreaming that they are still pressed to their mother, feeding. Jesse wipes his eyes on his sleeve. He could take them to his mother's old aunt, Nancy Gerrity. Nancy keeps all kinds of animals people bring her. If they are injured she nurses them to health, then, if they are wild, she releases them into the bush. Last time he saw her yard it was a grim, ramshackle place, with packing-crate hutches, and everything roofed with battered sheets of corrugated iron and fastened with a twist of wire. But no grimmer than starving to death out here for lack of milk, and anyway, animals don't care what things look like, as long as they're fed.

When he was a kid, he used to be scared when his mother would take him to Nancy Gerrity's place. Nancy's son Dale had been thrown from a horse and killed when he was twelve or thirteen – it had been years ago, before Jesse was born. Dale had been an only child. When Jesse visited, he'd felt bad for being a kid who had survived, while their son was in the cemetery. He'd told his mother he hated going there and she'd said he shouldn't, because Aunt Nancy was always happy to see him.

"After Dale died," Freddie told him, "my brother Don used to go over and help around the yard with the animals. Of course, he couldn't ever replace Dale, but he did his best, and Nancy and George loved him for it." Freddie had sighed and made a sad shape with her mouth.

"So what happened?"

"After a while, our mother told Don he couldn't go there anymore. Aunt Nancy never forgave her for that."

Jesse shakes his head, trying to free himself of these ancient family battles. But the past does cling, and he knows that it has subtly shaped them all in ways he cannot envisage or explain. He thinks of Miss James, her gentle demeanour. Miss James would give him the thumbs up if he chose to rescue these fox cubs. He doesn't doubt that she would believe in their purpose and their right to live.

It is warm, but with the pups in his pockets Jesse can't take off the hoodie. When he reaches the car, he leans into it for his phone. He swigs the last of his water and sets off towards the highway. Behind him the sun slants over the hill, and the trees and bushes throw down long shadows.

# THE TOWER

On the warm spring afternoons, nudged towards sleep by the slow drift of clouds past the tower's narrow windows, Dorelia's grip on the present loosened. Her roles as wife and mother, the burden of domesticity, which at times she had resented as sorely as if she had been 'in service', might never have existed; in the calm of those afternoons it was even possible to rise above the loss of Geordie. In the tower, it seemed as if she might live on more or less indefinitely; she might age without discomfort. It was an illusion, of course, but that was how it felt from the vantage point of her blue wing chair – her throne, as Bunty had dubbed it.

Dorelia thought of the medieval round tower she and Geordie had seen in Ireland. Its door was placed high up, to be reached only by ladders that could be retracted once all the villagers had taken shelter inside. Likewise, her tower was a solid refuge; it was a stronghold as private as memory.

One silent dusk, Dorelia found herself skimming back fifty years to a boat moored in the harbour at St Malo in Brittany. It was a June morning with sunlight snapping like scissors at the white blaze of the marina crammed with yachts. She was lying among rumpled sheets on the bed in the forward cabin, staring sleepily out of the porthole, while in the cockpit Bunty argued with Amos Hatherly. The people from the boat moored alongside had crossed their deck to reach the quay and several of them had dared to step on the guard rails. Instead of asking them to desist, Amos had rushed out of the wheelhouse, shouting. Elizabeth thought him rude and was telling him so. Dorelia could imagine Amos's dark features compressed with displeasure, his body quivering as it did when he flew into a passion, and she was glad to be out of the way.

That sleek white boat, the *Phaedra*, had belonged to Amos's father, a wealthy Mancunian. Elizabeth had met Amos at the art school in Paris, and by the time Dorelia arrived it had already been decided that the three of them would spend the summer painting together in Brittany. They had settled on St Malo because Amos's father had asked him to move the *Phaedra* to new moorings and oversee some minor repairs. They could live on the boat. Amos promised it would be perfect.

In Elizabeth's letters Amos's name hadn't cropped up once. Dorelia interpreted this censoring as a sign of his importance and was aggrieved that the summer she had been looking forward to for months had been appropriated by this unknown Englishman.

In the tower, Dorelia closed her eyes and allowed herself to sink into the memory of Amos Hatherly – his sharp, fine face, his long white body. She hadn't thought about Amos in a long time, had been scrupulous in not doing so, but with Geordie gone it no longer felt like a betrayal.

Amos had played the figure of the artist to the hilt, with his Claude Monet beard and his pale, paint-stained, linen suits. Out of doors he wore a white straw Panama, or the broad-brimmed Akubra he'd unearthed among Elizabeth's belongings. When Dorelia thought of Amos it was his energy she remembered, his drive to cram as much into every hour as he possibly could. Looking back, it was clear he had foreseen the burdens he would soon be called upon to shoulder in the cramped and dusty years that lay ahead. But in the charged atmosphere of that summer, the future had not yet been tainted for any of them by duty or disappointment. They could live as they wished, freed by distance from the judgements of their families and from the disapproval of the societies they had sprung from and would eventually return to. And if they had gone further than they ought, the pain they had caused had been far outweighed by the pleasure – even Bunty had said so, and it was Bunty who had suffered most, Bunty who'd had to bear the consequences.

Those high curved granite walls of St Malo's Old Town had sheltered dozens of tiny bistros. In the evenings the three of them would wander out arm in arm in search of somewhere to dine, she and Elizabeth wearing pale cotton frocks, Amos in a Breton fisherman's smock he'd bought at a flea market. Each establishment had a few outside tables, some set with red-checked cloths, others bare, and there were jugs, or tall preserving jars, crammed with lilies.

The first time Dorelia saw one of those tables with its creamy flowers afloat in the dusk, her thoughts had flown back to Sydney and the unadorned streets where she had been raised. Sydney's beauty was all concentrated within its watery setting; no one she'd ever known had dreamt of filling a preserving jar with the long stems of lilies and setting it on a dining table. In the coffee houses she and Bunty frequented there might be a wax-encrusted wine bottle with a candle stuck in its neck, but in France, the casual beauty of everyday things had left her breathless.

It was strange the way these distant memories came so easily to her in the tower when more recent events were often difficult to grasp. As dusk dissolved into evening, Dorelia gave herself up to the past.

# ESPERINE

Nick and Mariel checked out of their Miami hotel without eating breakfast. They were hungover, and jetlagged, but mostly they were freaked out by the weirdness of America. They had arrived via a flight from London to Los Angeles. It was close to Easter, and in LA's domestic terminal, where they had waited for their onward flight, it seemed as if every second passenger had travelled with an animal. Mariel saw parrots and cats; lunging dogs of all shapes and sizes were let out of travel cages to cavort in the concourse among travellers waiting to reclaim their luggage. The star turn was a tattooed man with an iguana draped across his shoulders.

"These people are crazy," she'd whispered to Nick, and fleetingly she had thought of their house in East Sussex, snug among apple and pear trees and rose bushes. Her dog, Poppy, would be fretting in boarding kennels, and Mariel had wondered whether she was glad they'd come.

During the long-haul flight she had watched a CNN report about two British tourists who'd been fatally shot in a supermarket car park in Sarasota; according to the police there had been no motive. Mariel's sudden awareness of the presence of guns, coupled with the airport chaos, had made her uneasy, so that from the moment they emerged from the terminal building in Miami the city had felt charged with menace. A taxi driver with bundled dreadlocks had accosted them outside arrivals, snatching up their luggage and jamming it into the boot of his car, ignoring their protests. It was March 1983, and when Nick explained that they did not need a taxi because the hotel had promised to arrange their transfer, the man's laconic response would lodge in Mariel's memory for decades.

"They *lied*," he drawled.

From the airport to the hotel, his crackling radio broadcast an impassioned oration by Papa Doc, or Baby Doc, or some other Haitian politician. The night air had felt intimate and clammy; it had frizzed Mariel's hair. And later, when they'd left the hotel in search of somewhere to eat, they had discovered the prevalence of Spanish when everyone they'd approached for directions, including two policemen, had not understood their English. Crossing broad streets against the flow of right-side-of-the-road traffic, they were always looking the wrong way and had twice narrowly escaped being run down. With the CNN report still at the forefront of her mind, Mariel had urged a retreat to their hotel and the safety of a bar meal.

It would be better once they were out of the city she thought, as they loaded their luggage into the hire car. But navigating onto U.S. Highway 1 put them both in a sweat. All around them the traffic flowed so fast, and Mariel sat with the map of Florida unfolded in her lap trying not to let Nick see that she was frightened. They had drunk too much last night. Possibly Nick shouldn't even be driving. Mariel wondered whether he would pass a random breath test; she wondered whether he understood the road rules. She couldn't ask, couldn't question his ability to drive on what felt like the wrong side of the road in a left-hand-drive car.

There were moments of respite when the traffic lights turned red. But soon they were rushing forward again. Under cover of the map, Mariel curled an arm around her stomach. Last night in the bland hotel room, woozy with exhaustion and drink, she

## Esperine

and Nick had made love. Mariel had drunk just enough to block thoughts of others who had done the same in the king-size bed – it was the thing she hated about staying in hotels. They could have gone straight to sleep, but Mariel's chart showed she was approaching the mid-point of her cycle. When they flew home, if she were still not pregnant, there would be the ordeal of the fertility clinic.

It was not so much the prying into their sex life Mariel minded, but the medical men and their instruments coming between her and her child. Perhaps the longed-for wee life was already burrowing into a warm fold of her womb. In Mariel's mind this precious seedling resembled a botanical drawing she'd once seen of a rare golden pear, "Esperine", which meant hope. Esperine was the secret name she had given to their unborn child.

They were on their way to Saint Lucia to stay with Nick's parents. The side trip to Key West was a present to themselves, a romantic interlude before a month of living in someone else's house. They planned to stop for breakfast in the Upper Keys, and once the traffic had eased Nick kept her amused with his Bogart impressions. They joked about being hijacked by gangsters in a seedy Key Largo hotel.

"You could pass for a young Lauren Bacall," Nick said, and reached across to squeeze her hand.

Mariel saw then that he had known she was scared and had been grateful for her silence. She smiled at her husband, whose English complexion and guileless blue eyes made him the opposite of any character ever played by Bogart.

"That film was made in the 1940s," Mariel said. "I suppose it all looks different now."

But when they came to Key Largo it was quiet and a little rundown, still a place Humphrey Bogart might recognise.

Nick pulled into the deserted car park of a diner.

"Where are all the customers? Mariel said.

Nick rolled his eyes. "They're inside, being held hostage."

On the threshold Mariel hesitated, and Nick gave her arm a reassuring squeeze. There was a jukebox and a long red laminex counter with upholstered stools. They chose a booth where they could look out over a children's play area, while a tired young woman with bleached-blonde hair served them coffee and the Country Breakfast – scrambled eggs and bacon, with fried potatoes or hash browns and slabs of toasted bread.

"I should have ordered the pancakes," Mariel said, as she picked at the pale peaks of scrambled egg.

Nick was sipping a second coffee when she absently touched her earlobe and realised her pearl earrings were missing. If she had picked them up from the bedside table they would be in her ears. She might have put them in her purse – Mariel fumbled in her handbag, fingers searching. She hadn't picked them up: they were still at the hotel.

Nick's mother had given the earrings to Mariel with great ceremony on the night before her wedding. They were a McCloud family heirloom, passed down to brides of the eldest son. Why had she touched her ear, Mariel wondered? On some level she must already have been aware of the loss. Sticky with panic, she couldn't bring herself to admit her carelessness to Nick.

There was a public telephone near the toilets. Mariel called the hotel and was put through to housekeeping.

Elena steered her cleaning trolley into room 513. The guests had only stayed one night and left early, so with luck there would not be too much mess. Once the door was closed she slipped off her shoes and pulled on a pair of the hotel's complimentary slippers over her socks. Her method was always to start by stripping the bed, for even after a single night's occupancy the bed linen could be shockingly soiled. Not that she was a prude, but handling the sheets with their oddly placed lipstick smears and other more intimate stains made her feel unsavoury, a voyeur after the fact. And yet the marks were like magnets; always Elena looked them over with a cold, unwilling eye. She was drawn to the stories they told, though they tainted her with their presence, thrusting her into a world of nakedness and abandon, a world of monied pleasure she would never know, or understand. Because if she had wealth, what she would buy would be silence, leisure, days of solitude in her own little house. Elena pictured this dream home as a rustic cabin on the edge of a lake, or sometimes as a whitewashed cottage perched high above the sea. In either place, it was miles away from the dingy flat on Charles Street, which she shared with her Aunt Lucilla.

Elena tied back the curtains. If these guests had not pissed in the bed, or even shat in it, she would be grateful. Oh yes, people did those sorts of things in hotel rooms. She approached the bed with caution and began the stripping, almost too tired this morning even to tease out the story of the stains. Still, she had a quick look – oh, these two had been hard at it; there was the evidence at both ends of the bed. Maybe they were honeymooners.

Having bundled the sheets and the used towels into the laundry bag, the next task was to make herself coffee; regular sips of double-strength black Nescafe energised her aching back, her tired feet, her hands – before she started at the hotel, Elena had never imagined hands could tire.

The hotel work was too physical, the hours on her feet too long. Elena was tall and slender with long, fine bones; she had never broadened out like the women in her family back in Quilpé, stocky women who regularly did the work of pack horses, or donkeys. When she had finished cleaning, she would go down into the hotel laundry – washing, starching, ironing, folding – or into the kitchen to earn overtime scrubbing pots and pans. Not that she would ever let on to that fat, lazy Marta, her supervisor, that the work was too hard. If she ever complained to Marta she'd be out on her ear.

Elena emptied two sachets of Nescafe into a clean white cup; she poured on hot water and inhaled the scented steam. With the cup between her hands, she sat for a moment looking out the window where palm fronds whipped back and forth in the wind. At home in Quilpé the days would be growing cooler, while here the hurricane season wasn't far away.

As soon as she went to dust the bedside tables, Elena spotted the earrings. They lay in the shadow of the clock radio, which is why the guest must have overlooked them when she left. The pearls, dangling from little upside-down gold crowns, were large and had a lovely sheen. In the bathroom she washed them and dried them with a tissue. Elena weighed them in her palm; the pearls were probably fake, but her grandmother, Maria Gloria, had owned a brooch with a real pearl in it, and before it had to be sold she had shown Elena and her sisters how to prove whether a pearl was genuine.

Elena pressed one of the earrings into her mouth and at once its grit against her teeth told her the pearl was real. Because false pearls, like false people, were smooth and slippery. Elena leaned in to the mirror and hooked an earring into her pierced right ear; she tucked in a stray wisp of hair and then turned her head. The pearl's radiance lent a glow to her cheeks; its lustre reflected in her dark brown eyes.

For years Elena had felt unworthy of jewellery. She believed rich adornments accentuated a plain woman's plainness, that they were best suited to the young, the beautiful, who could hold their own against the glitter. Though by no means plain, if Elena had any claim to beauty it resided in her thick hair coiled in a graceful knot, in her velvet eyes and narrow wrists, her quick, shapely hands. The rest of her had been drained of freshness by the daily grind, and at twenty-nine Elena already saw herself as a ruin, with nothing to look forward to but an endless run of dirty hotel rooms, which she would have to clean.

Yet as she gazed at herself in the mirror, the feeling of worthlessness evaporated. She was not diminished by the pearls, and perhaps their dazzle was even a little bit deserved. Of course, she could take steps to return the earrings to their owner. At reception they would have a contact number. Elena leaned closer to her reflection until her breath clouded the glass. Then again, that woman, likely a newly-wed, though not a virgin, had been loving it up all night on crisp white cotton sheets, whereas in Charles Street Elena had slept, exhausted, between washed-thin bedlinen.

It was the stains that swung it: the owner of the earrings had a young virile husband, what more could she need? In the mirror, with the pearl earrings swinging from the petals of her earlobes, Elena looked as she had often pretended when she was a child: a *princesa muy linda, a princesa perfecta*.

In St Lucia, Bea McCloud squeezed her fingers into a fist and knocked on the door of the maid's room. From within came a startled gasp, clearly audible to Bea as she waited on the step with the sun on her back – a gasp, and then silence. It was early, but already warm. As a fair-skinned Englishwoman, Bea found the knockout temperatures in the afternoons oppressive, which was why she liked to make an early start. When the door stayed shut, she pressed her lips together in irritation: it was the second morning in a week that the girl had failed to rise on time, and it really was too annoying when there was so much to be done.

Bea flung the door wide, and there perched on the edge of her bunk was Loverlie. She was pulling on a Bob Marley T-shirt over her naked torso and didn't hurry to cover herself; unembarrassed, she appeared indifferent to Bea's appalled gaze.

"Sorry, Missus," said Loverlie, her black eyes blinking sleepily into the hot sunlight. "That damn clock. It be dead."

"Well, I want you up, quick," Bea said. She averted her eyes as the maid reached for her skirt and slipped it over her head.

The girl must be stuffing herself when no one was watching, Bea thought, for lately she was looking rather stout.

"There's lots to do today," she urged, but Loverlie continued to dress at her own sweet pace. You simply could not hurry these people! Inexplicably, this thought brought tears to Bea's eyes, and she turned and stared hard at the corner of the terrace, at the mango tree by the steps that was ripening two large mangoes. Nicholas and Mariel would be here at Easter and Bea wanted their room turned out, she wanted the shutters dusted, the bathroom scoured spotless, and their beds made up with fresh linen.

As well as preparations for their visit, there would be a run into Castries for supplies. Bea felt heavy at the prospect. She especially hated buying the fish Clive was so fond of, for you had to wait on the wharf until one of the fishing boats came in – again, it was always in their own sweet time. Bright vessels with outboard motors and ridiculous names like *Lover Boy* and *Big Daddy* would pull in whenever their skippers felt like it. The fish was sold straight from the wharf, weighed on enormous old brass scales. All fish cost the same for a pound, and when you pointed to the one you wanted the fisherman would slice it with a machete – you wouldn't argue with one of those fellows, not even if they were robbing you.

For Bea the hardest part of living abroad was knowing what to cook. At first she had left the catering to their maid, but the girl before Loverlie had fried everything with garlic, which Clive wouldn't tolerate. Loverlie had been no better, so Bea had taken over the cooking herself, which meant that it was not much of a holiday.

On top of her busy day – it could take hours to buy the fish – Mike Huffman and his lady friend were coming at six o'clock for drinks. Bea had been half-hoping all week that they would call and cancel, but they had not. She'd invited them in a moment of loneliness, even though the girl, Genevieve, was odd. It had been

*Esperine*

the thought of company – Clive, of course, never asked anyone to the house. If it weren't for her they would see no one, except Loverlie and young Peter who helped in the garden.

Loverlie was dressed now, sliding her feet into the sandals Bea had given her when it was clear that on her days off she was walking the five miles to the village in bare feet. It would kill Bea to walk in the afternoon heat. She supposed you had to be born to it.

"There are pancakes in the kitchen," she told Loverlie. "And as soon as you've eaten, we'll start on Mister Nicholas's room."

"We double-checked, Madam, but there was no earrings in 513." Marta was opening a foil-wrapped hot chicken on her desk, the phone cradled between chin and shoulder while she tore off a wing and a leg and set them on one side for her lunch. "Yes, of course I spoke with the girl who cleans on that floor! She found two toothbrushes and a black plastic comb in the bathroom of 513, and those items are right here in lost property if you would care to call and collect them." Marta licked grease from her fingers. On her ample bosom a badge read *Marta Rodriguez, Superintendent (Housekeeping)*.

The voice at the other end, though faint, was agitated, with tears pending, if Marta were not mistaken. Trouble was brewing for that little idiot Elena if this woman-who-could-not-keep-hold-of-her-earrings chose to pester the hotel management. Marta would not allow that to happen, because it would reflect badly on her: she must be seen to be in control of her staff.

"I'm absolutely sure, Madam. She's a long-term employee and completely trustworthy."

Miserable rats, they were, most of these girls who cleaned. Here one day and gone the next; Elena had stayed longer than most. Naturally, the girl had shaken her head when asked about the earrings, but almost certainly she had taken them home.

"She must have lost them somewhere else," Elena had told Marta. "There was nothing in the room, only the two toothbrushes and the comb. No earrings. *Nada!*"

They headed for Key West against the background shimmer of the ocean; a pale aquamarine, it was unlike any water they had ever seen. In the passenger seat, Mariel nursed her distress over the lost earrings. The woman at the hotel had sounded bored by her persistence, but Mariel had begged her to speak again with the maid who had cleaned their room.

"I could offer a reward," Mariel said. "What's her name?"

"Elena Morales, but like I said, she didn't find anything."

"I know I left them there," Mariel said weakly. "So please talk to her again. I'll call tomorrow."

The Marta woman had rung off, the finality in her voice leaving Mariel little hope. How was she to face Nick's mother! She could say she had left the earrings at home, but Nick knew she'd been wearing them on the flight. The loss made Mariel nauseous, and she resented the damage this might inflict on Esperine. A tiny seed needed stability and calm to thrive, and Mariel's anxiety roiled in her, so that she felt constantly on the verge of throwing up.

In Key West they checked in to a motel on Duval Street. After they had unpacked and showered, Mariel got out her guide book. The day had lost its shine, but since they were here there were things they should see. She had been keen to visit Hemingway's house before the loss of the earrings had dampened her enthusiasm.

Nick put his arms around her. "What's up, doll?' he drawled.

She couldn't tell him. Not yet. Instead, Mariel hid her face in his chest, and the tears that had been choking her burst through as laughter.

"You're a lousy actor," she said.

# Esperine

When Bea pictured Nicholas and Mariel emerging from one of the small planes that flew the route from Florida to the islands, she was elated one minute and wracked with anxiety the next. Some things that had been said during Nick's recent telephone calls had made her suspect that he and his wife were on the verge of announcing they intended to sell up in England and settle in Australia. Bea feared that they had planned this visit so as to break the news.

But Nick and Mariel had not long owned their house in Fairlight, and Mariel appeared besotted with it. She had invited Bea and Clive down to East Sussex to admire the garden, which was undeniably pretty – with its fruit trees and mature shrubs, its tiny patch of woodland. The house itself, though, had been a disappointment. Its cottagey dimensions hadn't appealed to Bea, though she had been careful not to say anything negative. Mariel's joy in it had filled her with relief, for with any luck her daughter-in-law would settle into English life; she would put down roots.

For a while after they moved in, there had been no talk of Australia. Bea's anxiety had ebbed, though it had not been entirely erased. More recently, though, Australia – the climate, the beaches, Mariel's family – had begun to surface in conversations oftener than Bea would have liked. Clive had always thought migration might be on the cards, but Nick was their only child: it would be cruel if he were to be lured to the other side of the world when she and Clive were not getting any younger. If only Nick had married a lovely English girl!

They were due the next evening, and Bea wished now that she had been kinder when Mariel had confided she was having trouble falling pregnant. It had been during that last visit before she and Clive flew to Saint Lucia; Bea had gone down for the weekend by train, leaving Clive in town, and Mariel had met her at the station on the Friday night. The two days had sped by, with a pub lunch at The Bell at Iden, a bracing walk on the Fire Hills at Fairlight, and some pleasant pottering in the shops in Rye. Nick had been in good form, and Mariel had been vivacious in that arty, casual way she had that Bea sometimes found interesting and at other times felt was peculiarly Australian. Then, on the Sunday evening, as they were about to set out for the station in Mariel's car, the girl had suddenly looked limp and begun to cry.

"I'm sorry," she'd blurted, "I'll have to run inside a moment. My period's just started."

When she slid back into the driver's seat, instead of setting off for the station, Mariel had turned to Bea and described what she and Nick had been going through over the past year – the gruelling medical tests, the waiting and hoping every month, the relentless disappointment. Bea nodded; she had already begun to suspect something of the sort. With Mariel's own mother dead, perhaps she had been looking to Bea for comfort; almost certainly she'd thought there would be sympathy, because she knew Bea was keen for grandchildren.

"How awful for you," Bea had said.

And then the possibility of losing Nick had driven her to say the words she now regretted. Mariel had opened a pathway for it with her own outburst of emotion, but even so, it would have been better to have kept her mouth shut.

"My friend Morag's daughter-in-law has been in the same situation for ever so many years," she said. She'd looked across at Mariel, tense behind the steering wheel, and her face had been pinched and ghostly white in the darkened car. "Morag refers to her as 'that barren bitch'," Bea said, "which I think is terribly harsh. It's not something I'd ever say."

Mariel had turned and gazed at her for a long moment in silence, then she'd started the car and driven in silence to the station.

## Esperine

They bumped down in Saint Lucia at night, and on the long drive from the airport, under an almost full moon, Mariel caught glimpses of the island's mountainous landscape. Bea and Clive had built their holiday home on the side of a steep hill at the northern tip of the island. It was a low white villa with wooden shutters in place of windows and as they drew up it looked unlit and uninviting, even a little forbidding.

In daylight they would discover the house was perfectly sited to catch maximum sunlight and cooling breezes. The bedrooms were built around an indoor garden that was almost entirely filled by a lobster-claw plant. At first Mariel would want to sketch the flowers, but in the end she saw them as repellent – something about their truly uncanny resemblance to claws and their fleshy, almost human, texture. Beyond the garden the living area opened onto a broad terrace, and this, Bea told them, was where they took their meals and spent their days.

The perfect blue sweep of the bay, with the pointed shape of an island laid against it like a child's drawing of an island, could not have been more enchanting. Perhaps after all it would be pleasant to sit here in the sun for a month, Mariel thought, though she was still wary of her mother-in-law.

On their second day, Clive said he would drive them to Marigot Bay so that they could get their bearings. They would set out straight after breakfast. Mariel sensed that Bea didn't want to leave the maid to carry out the household chores unsupervised, but Clive brushed over her reluctance; he rounded them all up, and once they were out in the countryside, Mariel was glad.

The rutted road wound around steep hillsides, and often they looked down into a swaying sea of palms. Tiny shacks were dotted among the green; some were pink or yellow, but most were plain bleached wood. On the roadside, children waved and offered hands of bananas for sale. Once, on rounding a corner, they passed a family taking a bath on the verge – the tin tub shared and the washing done standing up with a soapy sponge.

Bea had laughed and turned to Nick and Mariel. "These people simply don't care about privacy," she said. "They'll do anything, anywhere."

Mariel did not laugh. She felt the throb of a headache starting. By the time they returned to the house she was ready for an aspirin and an hour or two in their bedroom with the shutters closed. She was pouring a glass of water when Nick came in looking embarrassed.

"I'd stay in here, if I were you."

"What's up?"

He shrugged. "My mother's going off about something."

Mariel stretched out uneasily on the bed; she loathed domestic squabbles. Now that she was alerted to the disturbance she could hear Bea's raised voice in the kitchen and a hiccupping sound that could only be the maid crying.

It transpired that Clive kept his radio tuned to the BBC World Service, and in their absence Loverlie had changed it to a local station to listen to music while she mopped the floors.

Bea was still fuming at dinner.

"Reggae, she said it was. Clive wanted to turn her out on the spot for touching his things. In the end he didn't, because I told him I wouldn't know where to find another maid."

Mariel made the coffee and volunteered for the washing up, hoping this would make it easier when she slipped away early to bed. Even so, Bea came twice and spoke to her through the door to ask if she were all right.

"Fine, thanks," she said, "just tired after the long drive."

Mariel lay in the dark thinking about Elena Morales and how somewhere in Miami she was wearing Nick's family's heirloom earrings. When they'd returned the hire car, Mariel had hoped to slip into the hotel and speak to Marta. In the end they were cutting it fine to catch their flight, so she'd made a final phone call from the airport.

"Look, lady," Marta had said, "for the last time, we did not find your earrings. And it's no good keeping on ringing me, no good asking for that girl who cleaned your room. Elena Morales finished her employment here a couple days ago – said her auntie had died and she had to move away."

So that was the end of it, Mariel thought. Either on this trip, or on some future visit to them in Fairlight – certainly at Christmas – the subject of the earrings would be raised. Then, she would either have to lie, or admit that they were lost and take what was coming in the way of judgement and recrimination.

It was better to be born lucky than rich: this was the prevailing wisdom in Elena's family, though in her twenty-nine years she had never witnessed much in the way of luck. Her grandparents had the one stroke of good fortune that had allowed them to buy the small house in Quilpé, but ever since, even middling luck had been spread thin. This meant that certain of the offspring had always to be sent away to work so as to send money home, and Elena had thought herself fortunate to have escaped to Miami in the care of her Aunt Lucilla. But even this small luck had run out when her aunt had a fall in the street, and before the ambulance arrived, she'd expired.

Lucilla had never married, and her niece was the only member of her family who was on the spot after the heart attack. Elena had had to cope alone with the formalities of death and with the expense. Had it not been for the pearl earrings, the cost of burial would have been beyond her reach. But she'd got a good price from a jeweller and had not needed to seek a loan to pay the undertaker. Elena had arranged everything, including her aunt's name to be said during mass in the Cathedral of Saint Mary. Then she'd set about looking for somewhere else to live, for the tiny flat the two of them had shared was unaffordable on her wages, even with the crippling hours of overtime.

Elena put off telling her family of Lucilla's death. Once they knew she was unchaperoned, they would insist on her coming home. But there was no future for her in Quilpé, whereas here at least she had hope. Luck could find her. Life could change.

She easily found a room in a *residencia*. What was more difficult was clearing the flat of her aunt's belongings, for as well as Lucilla's job in housewares at Burdines, weekend shifts at a charity shop had turned her into a hoarder. With the landlord threatening, and her long hours at the hotel, Elena became desperate enough to box up everything she didn't want and put it out on the sidewalk. She had thought the neighbours might complain, but things vanished fast.

With one small cupboard still to clear, Elena caught a head cold and spent a Sunday in bed so as to be well enough for work on Monday. On the Sunday evening, dosed with lemon tea and aspirin, and anxious about the landlord calling, she opened the cupboard and began to sort the contents. Had the cold not slowed her, she would have bundled the lot into an empty carton. Instead, she removed items one by one, and at the back, under a jumble of second-hand scarves and gloves, she unearthed a child's music box – dirty, scuffed pink, with a twirling ballerina. It was a sorry looking object, but to Elena's astonishment a drawer concealed in the base of the box contained six gold rings and a necklace. They were so glittery: they had to be fake. But when Elena slipped one of the rings onto a finger, its stones caught the light and flashed blue fire.

Mariel waited for Loverlie with the car engine running. From Monday to Friday the maid slept in a tiny room attached to the laundry, but on Friday afternoons she returned to her family in the village of Gros Islet. Her sister looked after things at home in her absence. Mariel gathered such arrangements weren't unusual.

Before Mariel and Nick came, Loverlie had walked to and from the village. Her feet were scarred, the pale soles as tough as shoe-leather. She was fit, but Mariel had soon divined that

Loverlie was pregnant. This might have sent her into a decline, as sometimes happened when people she knew announced their happy news, but just now she felt the strong presence of Esperine. It gave her a sense of kinship with Loverlie, and she couldn't abide the thought of her walking in the heat.

Nick asked his father if they could borrow the car.

"Do you want me to drive?" Nick said.

"It isn't far. I'll be fine on my own."

Loverlie, it turned out, had been born on the French island of Martinique.

"Followed a no-good man across here and never left," she laughed. In the Martinique tradition she wore a checked cotton hat tied in two peaks.

"It's the way you tie it that tells your status," she told Mariel. "Like married, single, or hooked up with a man who is unsatisfactory."

The colours were reds, yellows and oranges, traditional to the tiny mountain village where she had been born.

"You should see that place!"

Laughter bubbled so readily from her that Mariel was envious.

"So moist and cool, so many flowers. The lady mayoress she like flowers and make sure there are plenty. Coming down the mornes towards the coast you look into palm tops, all emerald, with patches of pink lilies, pineapples, coconuts, all you can eat." Loverlie showed her beautiful teeth in a smile.

She made Mariel laugh with her story of the mongoose, imported into Martinique to clean up the snakes.

"Did it work?"

Loverlie rolled her eyes. "The mongoose ate a few snakes, but in a little while it turns out he prefer chicken!"

In Gros Islet, houses of silvered wood perched on stilts beside the powdery grey road. Loverlie's candy pink house was a startling splash of colour in an otherwise monochrome landscape. A young child came running from the house at the sound of the car. Her little bottom was bare beneath a washed-out T-shirt, and she burst into tears at the sight of her mother.

Loverlie laughed and swung the child onto her hip. "Aye aye aye, what a welcome!"

Clive was selling the house, Bea told them. It was to be a private sale, and the four of them had been invited to lunch with expat friends of the prospective purchaser. Bea was eager, both for the quick sale of the house – which meant that they could return to England in time for summer – and for lunch with the Lathams.

"Betty Latham," she said, "is straight out of the top drawer. I believe she even has a title from a previous marriage."

The Latham's house was older and less attractive than the McClouds' villa, and was furnished in a style Mariel mentally dubbed 'expat grotesque'. There were brass-topped tables, ivory knick-knacks, even a few moth-eaten trophies. She eyed with revulsion an umbrella stand that looked to have once been part of an elephant. Framed newspaper clippings, and black and white photographs, strategically displayed, showed Lady Latham in her heyday – carefully coiffured, creamy shoulders rising from the foam of expensive ball gowns. It was clear she had once been a celebrated beauty, but those days had long passed. Whip-thin, sun-damaged, and nicotine-shrivelled, she still carried herself like a woman used to receiving compliments. She'd have been a match for Clive, Mariel thought, unlike poor Bea, who spent her life placating.

The first awkwardness was the realisation that they had not been invited for lunch. Betty Latham led them past a dining-table at which only two places had been laid, and Bea's face, when she realised her mistake, was a picture of dismay and embarrassment. Mariel managed to conceal her grin – it was obvious that their hostess had been aware of Bea's misapprehension about lunch and had wordlessly resolved it.

They settled in with drinks, and the two men withdrew to discuss the house sale. Betty Latham sat back with a cigarette and a gin and tonic and turned her attention to Nick and Mariel.

"So, you're Australian," she said to Mariel. And then to Nick, "Have you any children?"

"Not yet," Nick said.

Betty turned back to Mariel, raising thin, pencilled brows. "Oh! Well, how long have you two been married?"

Her bluntness took Mariel by surprise. "Five years," she said, trapped under Betty's gaze.

"Five years! Well, that's quite long enough to have had a rollicking good time together – and couples do deserve to have that little extended honeymoon. But you know, you need to produce some grandchildren for poor Bea." She waved her cigarette in Bea's direction and waited for a complicit smile, which was instantly forthcoming. "I have to say, my dear Mariel, you're being *terribly* selfish!"

There was a roaring like surf in Mariel's ears. Bea was tittering in the background, but all Mariel could hear was an angry sea and all she could see was Betty's amused and rather cruel face. Did she know? Was she tormenting her on purpose? Was it because she was Australian?

There was a knife on the cheese board; it was thin, with a serrated edge and a wickedly pointed tip. Mariel imagined snatching it up and plunging it into Betty Latham's heart. She imagined the CNN report: *Tourist fatally stabs woman in a motiveless attack*. Mariel leaned toward the cheeseboard and picked up a biscuit.

"*Selfish*," Lady Betty repeated.

Nick stirred beside her, and Mariel feared he would reach for her hand. A comforting gesture from Nick would only confirm what Lady Betty suspected.

Mariel stood up and asked to use the bathroom.

"It's through the archway."

In the green-tiled gloom, crouched on the toilet bowl, Mariel felt the slow seep of blood. She hugged her stomach while it trickled out of her – Esperine – flushed away on a tide of provoked emotion. She covered her face with her hands, but she did not cry, for she would not return to that ugly room with red-rimmed eyes. If she could just leave without stabbing anyone to death, without sobbing.

Back in the living room, Bea and Lady Betty were discussing Mike Huffman and his peculiar girlfriend. The couple had gone to The Plantation for dinner with the McClouds, during the course of which Genevieve had left the restaurant and not returned. Betty lit another cigarette.

"She isn't the first of Mike's young women, and I'm sure she won't be the last."

The men re-joined them and the conversation moved away from the mysterious Genevieve, leaving Mariel disappointed that they would likely never meet.

On the way back, Clive took the longer route, pointing out places of interest, including a house the locals had nicknamed 'The Malta Hilton'. Its owner had recently been shot dead and the blood stain could still be seen on the marble floor in the hall, Bea said, though she hadn't seen it herself.

In the back seat, Mariel kept her composure in the sticky heat by imagining bluebells carpeting the wood at home. How precious everything in Fairlight would seem on their return – every tree, every leaf, every blade of grass. She closed her eyes and remembered the day she and Nick were married, and how on the way from Winchelsea Church to the reception they had passed a small tree in flames. Nick had barely glanced at it, but to Mariel it was such an ominous sight that she hadn't been able to tear her eyes away.

It was a little pear tree in an overgrown front garden. She had often noticed it and wished she could feed it and arrange to have it pruned. But the cottage had been rented, one tenant after another, and none of them had seemed to care about the tree. Stunted in its growth, it had been blown sideways by the prevailing wind; on the autumn day of their wedding, when the tree's leaves had been gold, vandals, or perhaps disgruntled tenants, had set it alight.

Twenty years later, whenever LA is mentioned, Mariel will picture an airport with cats and dogs, she will picture tattoos and an iguana. The mention of Miami will conjure the shabby interior of a cab and the unhinged ravings of Papa Doc screaming through a crackling radio. She will marvel at what sticks in the mind and what time erases. After twenty years she will have forgotten the pearl earrings, but not the aquamarine shimmer along the Florida Keys. By then she and Nick will be living in Australia, and Esperine will be a dream they shared, as vivid and tormenting as the tree in flames.

# THE TOWER

During Hannah's absence, her husband had decided to sort out his archive. Geoff had taken over the dining-room, emptying his filing cabinets onto the dining-table, so that when Hannah returned unexpectedly from Wellington, they had to eat at the breakfast bar in the kitchen. It could only accommodate two people, side by side, and while their sons Darcy and Max were happy to eat on their laps in front of the television, this was not something Hannah had ever encouraged. She believed shared meals were the glue that held the family together, although after her aborted trip she was no longer certain that holding it together was what she wanted, or that sitting down with Geoff and the boys to plates of stir-fried this and that, or even the ceremonial Sunday roast, was a strong enough adhesive.

Playing over in her head was the woman's voice that had answered when she rang Simon's mobile, her hesitant *Hello?* And then when Hannah had asked for Simon, the voice saying bleakly, *Simon? But Simon's dead, didn't you know?* There had been a long, tense pause, and then the woman had said sharply: *Who is this?* What on earth had she said? Hannah could hardly remember. Something about checking the citations for a conference paper, and halfway through her stumbling explanation there had been a sound like a hiss. Before she could finish, the woman had hung up.

Geoff was oblivious to his wife's anguish. Only sixteen-year-old Max sensed that his mother was not her usual self. Hannah saw it in the sidelong glances he aimed at her as she cleared the chaos in the laundry and the refrigerator.

"I was only gone a little over two weeks!" She pulled a face as she drew a bowl of leftover pasta from the back of the fridge.

"If you'd let us know, we'd have all pitched in before you got back," Geoff said cheerfully.

Hannah intercepted the pitying glance Max aimed at his father and she huddled over the sink, fearful that this son, who was so like her, would somehow divine her thoughts. Because she kept returning to the humiliation of having secretly purchased and packed special underwear. Not only underwear, but perfume. She had not dared bring those flimsy garments home; they were so unlike the functional pieces that filled the bureau drawers in their bedroom. Instead, she had bundled them into a supermarket bag and abandoned them in the public toilets at Wellington airport. Perhaps a cleaner would find the unworn haul and take it home, to be sold on eBay – if you could sell-on such things – or use the garments to galvanise her own sex life.

Hannah had kept the perfume: Guerlain's *L' Heure Bleue*. It had been so expensive that the thought of throwing it away made her nauseous. She'd bought it without testing it on her skin, dreaming only of Jean Rhys and of Parisian trysts. But when she'd sprayed it on her wrists, though interesting at first sniff, it had dried down to a powdery old woman's scent of dusty irises and violets.

To Geoff and the boys, Hannah had danced around the reasons she'd cut her research trip short. The library's archive was not as relevant to her work as she had hoped; she'd been worried about her mother selling up and moving house. Both were true, but neither would have brought her scuttling home early if she had not felt so utterly gutted. Remembering how she had waited for Simon to call, how she had compulsively checked her email, her cheeks flamed with distress. Was it true that he was dead? Or had he just stood her up? Had his wife found out and forced him to let her deal with Hannah? She had googled his name and the word 'obituary', but nothing had come up.

Hot flushes, she told Geoff. Perimenopause. It wasn't true. She was a few years off that yet, thank God. But when it came, *L' Heure Bleue* would suit her; it would become her signature scent.

Hannah ran hot water into the emptied crisper from the fridge and scrubbed at the dried-on sludge left by an over-ripe cucumber. What if Simon were not dead; what if he had been at the airport and had watched her emerge from the arrivals gate? He might have planned to surprise her by whisking her away to take up where they had reluctantly left off at the end of the conference two years earlier. His emails had spoken of making up for lost time. But she was into her forties now. What if he had seen her and fled? If that were true, it had never been more than a sordid fling. Hannah rinsed the dish cloth and gave it a vicious squeeze.

Max followed his mother up the stairs at his Gran's new house, trying to avoid looking at her shapely calves. He had watched her take delivery of the parcel, noted her furtive movements, and later searched for and found the empty packaging in the recycling. There had been two labels, torn into pieces. He'd fitted them together and read that they had been attached to a balconette bra and brief set by a label called Pleasure State. Google had shown him a young tanned woman posing with a sucked-in stomach, her breasts cupped in black lace and some satiny fabric. Squirming, he had flung the pieces into the wheelie bin. But that night in his bed he had thought about the young tanned woman in the picture, and it had been Grace Harvey from his maths class.

Max looked around the tower room, and one of the pictures on the wall, an oil painting of boats in a harbour, reminded him of a visit he'd once made with his mother to Elizabeth Bunting's flat when she had been sick. While Hannah had heated soup in the kitchen, he had wandered around inspecting the paintings. The naked men had made him snigger, but there was one portrait of a woman lying in the shell of a boat, her hand over the side trailing in the water, her yellow blouse unbuttoned to expose her breasts to the sun. Something about the face was familiar. He'd been studying it with a gnawing sense of recognition, when Bunty appeared, hunched and pale, clutching an old kimono around her bony shoulders.

"Do you like this one?" she'd croaked.

Max had felt his cheeks redden as he nodded.

Bunty had leaned close to the painting and pressed a fingertip to the signature. "It's your grandmother," she said, "in France."

He hadn't known what to say, and to escape the old woman's gaze Max had turned to another, less confronting picture – a pot of waxy white hyacinths on a broad windowsill, with a scrap of lace curtain and the dark blur of distant trees. But when Bunty had tottered away, he had taken another furtive peep at the woman in the boat: her skin was tanned all over, with no marks from any swimming costume. Max wondered whether the artist, *A. Hatherly*, had painted out the tan lines, or whether his grandmother really had sun-baked naked in France, a thing which seemed impossible.

Looking at Dorelia sitting in her wing chair while the family trooped up and down the stairs, Max saw that she was anxious to have the room to herself; she didn't want them in it. He felt a fizz of interest, tinged with an emotion he had no clue how to express. His grandmother's hands were folded into the nest of her lap like two small birds; her feet in black court shoes shifted occasionally on the rug, betraying her impatience. It was fascinating, and appalling, to think that she would soon die, that her hands and feet, her soft cheeks and silvery hair, would be reduced to ash, which his mother and her siblings would carry away to the sea, or the mountains, to be ceremoniously scattered. There would be wine and tears, and his aunt would bring velvet cupcakes. That is what they had wanted to do with his grandpa, only his gran had refused. When she was gone, there would be no one to stop them. Max's curious gaze wandered to a small corner cupboard; books were stacked on top of it, and beside the books were three pink tulips in a green glass vase. Their loosened petals threatened to fall. Could that cupboard be where she kept his grandfather's remains?

"Have you made any headway with your mother about the dog?" Dorelia asked.

Max checked to see whether Hannah was within earshot, but she had gone downstairs.

"Mum says she won't clean up after a dog ever again, since our old dog became incontinent. I've told her I will do it, but she doesn't believe me."

His grandmother nodded. Max couldn't tell whether she was agreeing with his mother, or sympathising with him, but the injustice of it forced him to go on.

"The thing is, Trixie was already quite old when I was born, so I never had the best of her. I really want my own dog."

"Whose side is your dad on?"

He pulled a face. "I think they're on the same side. Neither of them are animal lovers."

"Well, taking on any living thing is a big responsibility, Max. Maybe your mother isn't ready for any more of that than she already has in her life."

His Aunt Gwen came in then, with her new girlfriend Mel. Max thought Gwen had struck lucky because Mel had a dog, even if it was a Yorkshire terrier.

On the way home, sitting in the back seat beside Darcy while his parents talked absolute rubbish in the front, Max wondered whether to have one last try at changing his mother's mind about the dog. If she still said no, which she probably would, he could mention the Pleasure State labels. He was certain his dad didn't know about the underwear, and although it would be excruciating to raise such a topic, Max sensed it had the power to win him a puppy.

# THE LITTLE FLOWER

"He'd be really old by now, that's if he's still alive," Kat said.

Sheena knew she meant the man who had raped and murdered Flora Helsden. For years the two of them had thought it must be someone they had seen around town all their lives; a man who had watched them walking to and from school, who had perved on them from behind sunglasses at the swimming baths. As children they had believed in his lurking presence because their mothers had had the story of Flora's murder drummed into them as girls. Sheena and Kat had been warned over and over never to be out on their own after dark, never to get into a car with a stranger. And yet whoever had done it wouldn't be a stranger, that was the scary part.

Flora would have been a good age, too, if she hadn't been strangled and her body left half naked on the football oval. The times walking home from school they had made a detour just to look at the place. Harmless, it seemed, its grass withered and yellow in the thudding heat of a summer's afternoon. One spring, in school uniform, Sheena had stretched out on the spot with her arms flung wide, seeing how it would feel to be Flora. She'd held her breath as if dead and felt the earth at her back – warm and moist, reeking of fertiliser and dog pee. The sky had pressed down hard with its blue, and she had jumped up in fright, her heart pumping. Every winter she and Kat watched brothers and cousins play football on the oval and still it looked as ordinary as anywhere. Yet it was marked with an indelible stain, it had to be.

The murderer had taken Flora's earrings for a trophy, or so it was supposed, since the pair she'd been given for her seventeenth birthday was missing and had never been found on the oval, or anywhere in the town. They were marcasite scallop shells, each with a tiny cultured pearl.

Flora Helsden had been Kat's great aunt. She had died only two hundred yards from her own front door, and her unsolved murder had cast a long shadow over the Helsden family. While the rest of the town appeared to have forgotten what had happened after a football club dance all those years ago, the Helsdens took it as their duty to remember. On the anniversary of Flora's death Kat and her mother always laid a floral wreath at the oval and took flowers to the cemetery. Now the anniversary was coming up, and Kat's mother was weak from her chemo.

"I'll come with you," Sheena said. "We'll do it together."

It was a Friday, and they were on their afternoon break, which they weren't meant to take at the same time, but The Little Flower Café and Collectables was empty, and the owner, Dot Letlow, had sent them out together. Beside the café, two white plastic chairs stood in the shade of a vine-covered pergola. This was where the girls carried their coffee in takeaway cups, where they could smoke without drawing disapproving looks.

Kat took a pack of cigarettes from the front pocket of her overall.

"It'll be fifty years," she said. "It's on a Friday, too, so we'll have to ask Dot for the morning off."

"She won't mind, if we tell her what it's for."

Though Sheena and Kat both worked at The Little Flower, it was only on Thursdays and Fridays that their shifts coincided. Sheena, who had recently abandoned her hairdressing apprenticeship, worked every day, while Kat made up her hours with another part-time job at Beale's newsagency. The two were saving up to move to Adelaide. Ever since high school, they had been planning their escape.

"If Bernard was old," Kat said, "you might think it was him."

Sheena squinted through a plume of smoke, ticks of black eyeliner at the corners of her eyes giving her a startled look.

"I know," she said. "The creep."

She ran a hand through her pale pink bob, and the pastel colour together with the light green café overall Sheena wore gave her the look of a delicate botanical specimen. Kat was shorter and heavier, with solid curves and a bundle of fiercely red hair done up on top of her head in a bun. Since her mother's illness she had taken on more at home, and with working two jobs Kat looked washed out in the greenish light under the vine. Even so, Sheena knew better than to suggest they skip the anniversary. In Kat's family it was a thing that had always been done and always would be done, as long as there was someone to buy flowers.

"I'll ask Dot about the time off," Kat said.

It was the anniversary of her father's accident that pressed uneasily upon Sheena's family. He had crashed his motorbike into a tree one morning on the racecourse road, and there weren't more than two or three trees along that whole straight stretch of tarmac. Mostly it was scrubby bushes, or patches of bare red soil. People said he must have swerved to avoid one of the feral goats that graze the verges. For her mother's sake, and for her brother Jesse's, Sheena always went along with this version of events. Still, the accident troubled her, and it was connected in her mind with something she had witnessed in the weeks leading up to her father's death.

She had arrived home in the middle of the day after slipping out of the school swimming carnival; her plan was to dump her uniform, then walk to the abandoned tennis courts behind the old farrier's workshop on Thomas Street and hang out there until home time. Her Uncle Jordan's car was in the carport beside her mother's white Toyota, and as she had passed the open kitchen window, Sheena had heard him saying goodbye. And then she'd glanced in and seen him give her mother a kiss, though not on the cheek like he would have at a family get together. Jordan's mouth was on Freddie's neck and her body had curved towards him. It had happened so swiftly, yet to Sheena it went on and on. When Jordan left the kitchen, Freddie had raised her fingers to the place on her neck where his mouth had rested. Sheena had decided then to risk the uniform and had bolted out the back gate.

This scene, and the uncertainty around her father's death, were things Sheena wanted not to have to think about once she left the town. Luscious Locks Salon was something else she looked forward to leaving behind. Luckily it was at the other end of the main street from The Little Flower, so she didn't have to walk past the windows and see Bernard's spidery body hovering behind a client as he blow-dried their hair. She pitied his wife Pixie, even though Pixie had made no bones about what she thought of an apprentice who would quit without warning. But it was better that Pixie was furious with her for leaving than for her to hear that her husband had smoked a joint in between customers, then pinned Sheena in the back room where they made tea and coffee and ground his hips against her. She'd struggled to push him away, for although Bernard was wiry, he was strong. She supposed he was handsome in a foreign-looking way; his female clients flirted madly with him, and Pixie thought there was no harm in it, that the flirting was good for business. But behind his wife's back he would creep up on Sheena, or the part-time colourist, Leah; he'd slide his hand up under their shirts, or try to kiss them. Probably he did it to other women.

Sheena didn't mind serving in the café at The Little Flower, but best of all she liked unpacking the second-hand stock — books, old china, vinyl records, odds and ends of costume jewellery that she would scrub clean with hot soapy water and an old toothbrush. She liked arranging displays on the glass shelves in the café window, and in the side room that had a few café tables as well as the bookshelves filled with bric-a-brac. The china cups and plates looked as good as new when they'd been washed and polished, as did the glassware when she'd buffed it with a cloth. Sheena had bought a few pretty cups and saucers for when she and Kat had their own place in Adelaide. Her mother thought she was collecting them for her glory box, but Sheena and Kat had sworn a solemn oath never to marry anyone from the town. If either of them was tempted it would be up to the other to make the smitten one see sense. They took this pact seriously.

Not that Sheena was in any immediate danger, for after the experience with Bernard any man who made overtures was given short shrift. Kat was amenable to dating, so long as the blokes she went out with knew not to get serious. In the meantime, there was Kat's mother with breast cancer. Privately, Sheena thought this was likely to be more of an obstacle to Kat leaving town than Dan Beale the newsagent's son who phoned her every night, or the young policeman, Ted Capelli, who brought her jars of his mother's home-made pasta sauce. Next thing, he would be inviting her to meet his parents. Kat only laughed and said if he ever did she wasn't going.

Dot and Dave Letlow owned The Little Flower. They'd arrived from Sydney, the town having stuck in their minds from a road trip they'd taken together when they were teenagers. Some trauma they had suffered in the city had prompted them to uproot their lives, to try and rewind to a time when they'd been a couple of young hippies passing through a place they'd remembered as slow-paced, a town with old-fashioned values. Dave suffered from depression, Dot said; he'd been in therapy. A tall man, with shaggy, greying hair, he took little part in the day-to-day business of the café.

Dot Letlow was a large, energetic woman, with an impressive memory, so that customers who'd come in once for tea and cake would be greeted by name at their next appearance. Most of them seemed to lap up the familiarity, though it made Sheena squirm. After a lifetime in the town she looked forward to a city's anonymity, the knowledge that no one would know where she was or what she was doing. She could be up at the crack of dawn, or lie in bed all day eating toast and reading. There would be no one to nag.

*Josephine Anne Clooney, a married woman residing at Bent Street, said the deceased, Flora May Helsden was her younger sister. On the evening of September 1st, the deceased called at her home and said she was on her way to a dance at the football club. Flora Helsden was in good health and spirits when she left the witness's house. Josephine Clooney identified a pair of gloves and a handkerchief as belonging to her sister. They were found on the railway line, about eighty yards from the scene of the crime. She also identified a lipstick, saying she had watched her sister applying it to her mouth. The lipstick was said to be of an indelible variety, which meant it would not smear.*

*Flora Helsden apparently left the football club during the medleys; the Pride of Erin was playing when she went shortly before midnight. A friend noticed her walking alone along Stead Street and then towards her home. She was not seen alive again. Detectives are not losing sight of the fact that she might have been followed from the dance hall.*

Sheena and Kat were looking through the book of newspaper clippings that had been kept in Kat's family since the time of the murder. They were in the kitchen, while Kat's mother Ros lay on a sofa in the living room with the television's volume turned down low.

*William Terence Gurney, a pipefitter, residing at Bent Street, said that at 6.45 a.m. on September 2nd he was walking along the railway lines in a southerly direction. He said he found a pair of gloves and a handkerchief in the middle of the lines. The handkerchief was over the gloves, which were rolled together.*

*The victim was buried today in the Catholic Cemetery following a Requiem Mass at the cathedral. A large number of people attended the funeral and many more lined the route, bowing their heads as the cortege passed.*

*A leading florist said that she had been unable to fulfil a contract for fifty wreaths. Flowers, ordered from Adelaide, were offloaded from the plane, but she could only complete ten out of the fifty wreaths. Other florists in the town were also short of flowers.*

There was to be a dance at the football club on the Saturday night following the anniversary. Kat wanted to go, but Sheena wasn't keen.

"What can possibly be the point?"

Kat poured them each a glass of white wine. "A fiftieth anniversary," she said. "If you'd murdered someone would you be able to resist going back for a wander down memory lane?"

"I would," Sheena said. "Because I'd stick out like a spare prick among all those teenagers."

"We'll stick out a bit ourselves," Kat said.

"So, let's do the flower thing and leave it."

Kat's mouth was pressed into a determined line, and when she looked like that, resistance was useless.

"Oh, all right," Sheena said. "I'll come and keep an eye on you."

A cold wind was blowing across the oval on Friday morning. The grass was damp and their heels sank into it, as they made their way to the spot by the fence where Flora's body had been discovered. Kat carried a wreath of pink roses from which a heart-shaped card protruded: *In loving memory of Flora Helsden, cruelly taken, never forgotten.* A man walking a greyhound stared at them as they settled the wreath on the grass. A woman in orange leggings was running up and down the steps of the grandstand; the spaces where people parked to watch football matches were empty. They put a bunch of white lilies into the back seat of Kat's mother's car and drove out towards the cemetery. The perfume from the flowers was strong, and Sheena's head began to throb: she wound down her window a bit.

"What time did you tell Dot we'd be in?" she said.

"Around ten."

The cemetery was deserted. A light breeze blew Sheena's hair into her eyes, and she wished she'd worn flatter shoes. Flora's grave had a white marble headstone surmounted by a marble cross; the cross was decorated with a wreath of marble roses. It stood a little apart from the surrounding graves, as if those buried there hadn't wanted to be tainted by her violent death. Kat had brought a dustpan and brush and a bottle of water from the car, and while Sheena filled a vase and arranged the lilies, Kat brushed away dirt and dead leaves and made everything tidy. Sheena kept an eye out in case anyone might be lurking, but the only movement was the wind.

Her father was buried in another part of the cemetery. She hadn't visited his grave since the funeral, and knowing he was there made her uncomfortable. Before she left town she would go; she'd take Jesse and her mother and they'd make sure the grave was tidy, as Kat was doing for poor Flora. Part of her mind began to dwell on how lonely it would be out here among the dead, waiting day after day for someone to pick up the empty beer cans and vodka bottles that were strewn around and to lay fresh flowers. Another part wanted to nip this sentiment in the bud. Because when you were dead you didn't wait for anything, you were oblivious to the living world.

## The Little Flower

Football club dances had changed since Flora Helsden's time. For one thing, there were no musicians and no Pride of Erin. A DJ had set up his equipment at one end of the long narrow clubhouse and there was a bar at the other. The walls were crowded with team photographs from the club's earliest years up to the present, and there were flags and signed football guernseys. The names of Best and Fairest players were inscribed in gold on a honey-coloured slab of wood. The club's colours were brown and gold: they had always been the Hawks.

Kat and Sheena ordered glasses of white wine. The dance floor was packed with young people moving in time to the music; coloured lights pulsed, and faces shone with sweat. Kat nudged Sheena towards a pair of vacant stools, and they sat at the bar with their drinks. Between sips, Sheena turned and peered into the crowd, but there was no one on the dance floor older than about twenty, nor was there anyone even middle-aged in sight except two men on the door, who would be football dads, and two women behind the bar, who would be football mums. There was no one of an age to have been young when Flora Helsden had danced here wearing indelible lipstick. Around the edges of the dance floor, groups of girls stood giggling. Sheena remembered such evenings from her own late-teenage years, the uncertain dynamics, the ridiculous crushes and crude manoeuvring.

In the entrance, two young uniformed policemen stood talking to the football dads. One of them was Ted Capelli.

Sheena said to Kat, "Your Italian admirer has come looking for you."

Kat sat up straighter on her stool. "It's a working visit," she said. "I don't suppose he expected to find me here."

But Ted had already spotted them at the bar; he was staring across the crowd at Kat, his black eyes beady.

*Michael Colin Dawney, a miner, residing at the Zinc Barracks, said that he had been taking Miss Helsden out for the last six or seven months and that he was known to her as Mickey. Dawney said that he was out with Miss Helsden the night before she was murdered. He had not been at the dance on the night of the murder, though he had attended on previous occasions. He had not known Miss Helsden was going to the dance that night.*

*To Sgt. Milner: I regarded myself as her boyfriend, and if I had known she went out with anyone else I would have resented it. To my knowledge she had not been out with other boys while I was friendly with her.*

Kat went to have a word with Ted Capelli. There was a slow dance in progress, and Sheena watched couples shuffling towards the darkest spots on the dance floor, clinging to each other with clammy hands. It would have been like this on the night Flora was murdered and on countless nights since – girls in their best frocks with their eye makeup melting, the boys they danced with already hardening into men. She wondered if Mickey Dawney had somehow discovered that Flora was at the dance that night. He might have arrived without warning during the last slow waltz before the Pride of Erin; he could have hovered in the doorway where Ted Capelli stood now with Kat. Sheena thought of her uncle, Jordan Barry, his mouth on her mother's neck. It would only take the slightest thing to make someone snap – figures glimpsed through a window; a remark overheard in a bar.

The photographs of Flora in the newspaper showed a dark-haired girl with bright dark eyes. She'd been pretty; friends had described her temperament as 'lively', her character as 'good'. Maybe all Flora had done to bring about her own death was to dance a slow waltz.

Three months after the football club dance, at The Little Flower Café, ropes of tinsel looped across the ceiling and swayed in the draught from the air conditioner; a Christmas tree twinkled with coloured lights in the front window. Every day was busy, and the bric-a-brac was selling fast. Sheena set up new displays every morning, washing and polishing china and glassware to replace pieces that were sold, sorting through the boxes of costume jewellery Dot had bought at the weekly auction mart. She had tried different methods of cleaning jewellery, and now as well as hot soapy water she used baking soda and salt with aluminium foil to remove tarnish, or she'd use toothpaste, or vinegar. Marcasite pieces she buffed with a silver cloth.

In the bottom of one of the boxes, under a tangle of beads, Sheena found a pair of marcasite screw-back earrings in the shape of scallop shells. In each shell nestled a tiny pearl. Sheena held them on her palm, and the stuffy little back room where she sorted the stock seemed momentarily cold. The earrings were like those that had been worn by Flora Helsden. There had been a photograph of them in the old newspaper clippings. What if whoever had taken them from her body had finally died and their belongings had ended up in the auction mart?

She spoke to Dot about the earrings, and to Kat. With Dot's permission, Kat rang the police station and asked to speak to Ted Capelli, and an hour or so later, he and another police officer arrived at The Little Flower.

Sheena had put the earrings into a small white cardboard box. Ted studied them carefully and then looked at Kat.

"And you say these are the same design as the ones that girl was wearing in the book of clippings you showed me?"

Kat nodded. "And look, no one wears screw-backs these days. They have to be the right era."

Ted said he would write a report and make enquiries at the auction mart.

When Sheena and Kat got to Adelaide, they planned to stay at a backpacker's hostel while they looked for work and somewhere to live. Sheena's mother had cried when she told her she was saving up to go. Kat's mother had already known. Luckily Ros was over the worst of her treatment and had returned to her job at the Credit Union. In the meantime, Kat had given in her notice at Beales and was working extra shifts for Dot. Only Ted Capelli had tried to talk Kat out of leaving.

On New Year's Eve, Ted called at The Little Flower to speak to Dot Letlow before she closed the café. Sheena and Kat had finished putting chairs up on tables and hovered at Dot's side to listen.

The earrings would stay on file with the police, though Ted's superiors were pessimistic about an outcome.

"It's difficult," he said, "with nearly everyone from that time having passed on."

Dot shook her head. "A girl was murdered," she said. "She might have passed, but she hasn't gone away. People in the town remember."

Ted said he was checking on everyone in the last few months who had taken second-hand goods to the mart. One of his colleagues was combing through the newspaper obituaries.

"It could be that someone who died recently had a connection with the case."

Ted turned towards Kat, and his eyes glistened with reproach.

Sheena found she was holding her breath. Flora Helsden must have known her killer. He'd followed her from the dance, or he'd come from a pub and bumped into her walking home. She wondered why Flora would go to the house of her married sister to put on lipstick, to dab perfume behind her ears and fix her hair in the hall mirror: the house was not on the way to the dance. She saw again her own kitchen and Jordan Barry's mouth on her mother's neck. All these years, someone had kept Flora's earrings. A girl could die for such little things.

# THE TOWER

Unchaperoned on the *Phaedra*, Dorelia and Elizabeth had believed themselves daringly modern. In Paris, Amos and Elizabeth had been lovers, and now amid the intimacy of their living arrangements, intoxicated by jars of white lilies and by their newfound freedom, Dorelia's antagonism towards Amos dissolved, and she, too, fell under his spell.

Elizabeth was not jealous, or possessive, so that when Amos asked Dorelia to pose for him in the ruined shell of a dinghy he had found abandoned along the shoreline, she packed her paints and set off cheerfully on a series of solo expeditions. It was during the painting of that picture, Amos's finest achievement of the summer, that he and Dorelia grew close.

It ought to have felt strange, their triangular affair, but for Dorelia it was an extension of the steadfast affection she had always felt for Elizabeth, so that loving her with and through Amos was merely a novel variation. The three of them drank copiously in the evenings, which was another novelty, since none of the women in Dorelia's family had ever touched alcohol, and even the female art students she'd known had mostly stuck to coffee and soft drinks. On board the *Phaedra* they drank *chouchen* made from fermented honey, or the lightly sparkling Breton cider. At dinner in the Old Town there was wine, and brandy, with the walk back to the boat unfolding in a whirling, unsteady blur.

Dorelia had thought their loving selfless; she believed it would benefit her art. But those high-blown ideas had been rubbish: they had just been young, and wild for new experiences, and if Amos had used them, they had used him, too, for their mutual pleasure.

"My beautiful muses," he had called them, opening his arms to embrace them, one arm for each.

But he had been their muse, too, and their collective energy had generated a frenzy of new work, some of it extraordinary. They had painted each other painting, sleeping, eating, bathing; for weeks they painted *en plein air*, roaming the Breton countryside to set up their easels. At times they covered great distances, yet never grew tired.

It was only as the summer waned that Dorelia had begun to suspect this was to be the extent of Amos's life as an artist. A comment here and there, certain overheard conversations between him and Elizabeth, led her to realise that when the summer was over Amos would return to Manchester and take up a position in his father's factory.

Dorelia had been saddened by this, because Amos Hatherly was a wonderful painter. Not gifted like Elizabeth, but with time, who knew what he might have become.

# MONKEY PUZZLE

In the lounge of the Sunny Days Aged Care Home, Lydia Flewett sat poring over the pages of the local newspaper. Ever since she had moved into care this daily sifting of the news had been an almost sacred ritual, although as time went on the reading required more and more concentration. Still, by focusing closely on the task, she was usually able to gather some titbits of news that would engage the attention of the handful of residents who, like herself, were not too far sunk in dementia to show an interest in the ongoing life of the town. One or two of them would even peruse the newspaper when she had finished with it, though Lydia suspected they were not really reading, just skimming the headlines.

After the upset there'd been, it was even more important to find something positive to chat about. Lydia was hoping for a good-news story – perhaps a lottery win for some deserving punter, or a fiftieth wedding anniversary. Her friend at Sunny Days, Ada Barlow, loved an anniversary, and of all of them it was poor Ada who had been most upset by that ugly scene in the common room. Lydia looked up from the newspaper, hoping her friend would appear with her walker. If Ada came and sat next to her Lydia could read out items of interest as she found them rather than having to hold them in her mind to tell later;

holding onto things these days was dicey, though so far she had been able to keep this knowledge to herself.

The lounge was quiet, with only Mr Lonergan parked in front of the windows in his wheelchair. A shrivelled old man, he'd once been chief stipe of the course in the days when Lydia and her husband Cyril had gone to the races. In his scarlet jacket and long black riding boots, Johnny Lonergan had cut an impressive figure on horseback. A big grey he used to ride; Lydia could see it dancing sideways as it came out through the gate onto the track. When she'd first arrived at Sunny Days, Mr Lonergan had been keen to discuss the racing news; dogs or horses, he'd never minded. But now nothing held his interest – indeed, he hardly recognised his own children when they came to visit.

Lydia sat up straighter on her chair and her soft pale face with its crumple of fine lines was momentarily apprehensive; her blue eyes darkened. It was the worst thing she could imagine: no longer knowing your own people. Cyril was long gone, of course, but her daughter Pixie came often. Lydia would sooner die than not recognise poor Pixie.

"A cup of tea, dear?"

The new young carer had come up quietly beside Lydia. Blessica, a Filipina so softly spoken that most of the residents never heard a word she said.

Lydia shook her head. "I think I'll wait for lunch."

After a quick look around the lounge, Blessica sat down beside Lydia.

"Those things I show you, from the old gentleman, Mr Clooney? After we look that time, I put back in his room," she said.

Lydia thought the girl looked quite frightened. She hadn't been on duty when Mr Clooney had collapsed during the film show, but she must have heard about it.

"I worry people think they stolen," Blessica said. "Maybe they not believe he insist to give me those things?"

Lydia considered this for a moment in silence. The girl had shown her the presents. Earrings, there'd been, and a rather pretty brooch, as well as something pink that she couldn't quite bring to mind.

"I think that was wise, dear," she said. "They might have been family treasures and Mr Clooney's children could come looking for them now that he's gone."

Blessica nodded, and the anxiety that puckered her face dissolved into a dazzling smile. She was a pretty girl, with shining dark hair drawn back into a single braid; the prettiness and the smile were doubtless the reason the presents had been pressed on her, Lydia thought. But there would be rules about that sort of thing at Sunny Days, and a junior staff member wouldn't want to fall foul of the woman in charge, Mrs Addison.

Lydia had watched Gladys Addison bend to feel for a pulse on old Mr Clooney's wrist after he had collapsed during the screening of *The Sound of Music.* Behind steel-rimmed spectacles, Mrs Addison's eyes were as cold and expressionless as a pair of frozen peas. When she had found no pulse, she had dropped the wrist into the old man's lap and called for the porters to ring an ambulance.

Poor Ada had been sitting next to Mr Clooney when he'd fallen sideways, pinning her to the vinyl sofa. A strangled gasp, and then he had been stone dead there in Ada's lap. You'd have thought Mrs Addison would have offered a word of comfort, but there'd been nothing said, not even a cup of tea brought for Ada after the porters had prised her out from underneath Mr Clooney.

Pixie Flewett sat hunched in her car in the Sip'n Save carpark. She'd had to pull in to let her breathing return to normal. The Fitbit she wore showed her elevated heart rate – it was the stress of what she had just seen and the realisation, finally, that she would have to divorce Bernard. He'd always flirted. Clients liked it, he said. But there was more to it than just the clients –

Bernard had never been able to leave the female staff alone; Pixie had guessed it was why their latest apprentice had walked out in the middle of a busy Friday.

Girls were one thing; they were almost a hazard of the job. But just now Pixie had run back into the salon for the photographs she'd promised to show her mother, and when she'd appeared in the tea room, Bernard and that slippery fellow Grant, the hair products rep, had leapt guiltily apart. Grant, weasel-thin in his blue business suit, was as camp as anything; one look at him and you'd know. Oh crikey, she'd thought, not boys, too! But yes, girls or boys, it made no difference to Bernard. Pixie had always had her suspicions.

The split would be expensive and ugly. She'd have to speak to Cecil Briggs, the solicitor who had drawn up her mother's will. Cecil was a dry old stick, but he would steer her safely through the divorce.

By the time she reached Sunny Days, Pixie was calmer. It would all be ghastly, but at least there were no children to be divided between them, only clients. Thank goodness she had kept her surname when she and Bernard married. She could open another salon on her own account. Pixie found her mother sitting in the sun lounge with a newspaper folded on the coffee table in front of her. For a moment, as Lydia Flewett's eyes came to rest on her, Pixie thought with alarm that they looked completely vacant.

"Mum? It's me," Pixie said anxiously.

Lydia came to with a little start. "Oh, of course it's you! Lovely to see you, dear."

Pixie sat down, and with her mother's habitually sweet-natured expression restored, a part of her longed to confide her troubles even though she had resolved on the way over not to mention Bernard, or divorce, until it was all in hand.

While Lydia started to tell her something that was in the newspaper, Pixie thought of how her mother had not been keen on her marrying Bernard. Nothing had ever been said against him, but there had been a distinct absence of enthusiasm. Over the years Bernard had tried to win her mother with his flattery, but there had been a gleam of scepticism in Lydia's gaze whenever it had settled on her son-in-law. Pixie felt certain her mother would not be distressed by the news, and again she felt the urge to tell.

"It was a very long time ago," Lydia was saying. "But the police are looking into the case."

"What's that, Mum?"

"That poor girl who was strangled and left on the oval after a football club dance. She was very young."

Pixie shook her head, and her long beachy waves rippled like a shampoo advertisement.

"There was something important," Lydia said. "It'll come to me in a minute."

Pixie fished the photographs from her handbag and began to flick through them.

"Leanne's wedding," she said. "I bought this dress last time I was in Adelaide."

"Beautiful!" Lydia smiled.

As Pixie held out each photograph for her inspection, Lydia was thinking how the New Look of her youth had been far more flattering than today's fashions, though of course you'd needed a narrower waist than any of these women in the photographs possessed. Lydia had been forty and still with a reasonable waistline when she'd fallen pregnant with Pixie. She and Cyril had long given up hope, and then suddenly they had been blessed with this baby girl. Now Pixie was forty-two! How those years had flown!

"Leanne's dress was stunning, don't you think?" Pixie said, gathering the photographs and returning them to her bag.

Lydia nodded. It was something in the newspaper that had started her thinking, a picture of a pair of marcasite earrings that had turned up in a second-hand shop. They'd all worn marcasite back then and yet nowadays you hardly saw it.

"There was something I wanted to ..." Lydia fumbled towards the thing she needed to tell Pixie. It was almost within her grasp.

"I'll come back on Sunday," Pixie said. "Take you out for a little drive."

Ada hadn't been the same since Mr Clooney had flopped into her lap. She was silent and withdrawn, and Lydia couldn't attract her attention.

"She poorly," Blessica crooned, when Lydia remarked that Ada was different. "But in a little while she be better."

Lydia wasn't optimistic. Since Ada's younger sister had moved up to Queensland, Ada no longer had visitors, and that old man dying like that seemed to have pushed her over some threshold. Instead of wheeling her walker across the sun lounge to sit beside Lydia, Ada now favoured a seat near the window. Mr Lonergan was close by in his wheelchair, but the two never spoke. Lydia's attempts at conversation were rebuffed, and Ada just stared out the window to where a monkey puzzle tree rose out of the lawn, its branches a complex pattern that reminded Lydia of the coral she and Cyril had seen once from a glass-bottomed boat on the Great Barrier Reef. But the branches of the monkey puzzle were not prettily coloured like coral. She found their crazy arrangement of stems and twigs disturbing.

Lydia had been in her first job when the girl's body was found on the oval. Fletcher's Photo Shop – she'd served behind the counter, but it was the darkroom work she'd loved best, a witness to the magic of images gradually appearing on the photographic paper. Everything in the town that was photographed in those days had passed through her hands, from dogs and horses winning races, to weddings, birthdays, and christenings. And because back then the police hadn't had their own photographer, on the morning the murdered girl's body had been discovered they had asked Des Fletcher to come down to the oval with his camera. Later that same day Lydia had stood beside him in the darkroom and watched the gruesome images materialise. Flora Helsden, the dead girl had been called. The top half of her body had been naked and there had been purple bite marks all over the poor girl's breasts.

Those earrings in the newspaper were like the ones Blessica had been given by Mr Clooney. Shells, each with a pearl. It was good that Blessica had returned them, thought Lydia, because they were probably quite valuable. The newspaper said the police were treating them as a clue to Flora's unsolved murder. Lydia waited anxiously for Pixie to come. Pixie knew everyone in the town, she could tell someone in the police about Mr Clooney having those earrings.

But on Sunday Pixie did not appear for the promised outing. Late in the afternoon there was a phone message for Lydia: her daughter was sorry, but she was coming down with a cold. By now Mr Clooney's room had been assigned to a new resident. Lydia wanted to ask what had happened to his belongings, but whenever Mrs Addison appeared, Lydia was daunted by her chilly manner. There was no one else Lydia could tell. She would have to wait for Pixie to get over her cold.

"A bit of a turn," said Mrs Addison. "She is not quite with us, if you know what I mean."

"No," Pixie said, "not really. Are you saying Mum's delirious?"

"Wandering a bit in her mind," said Gladys Addison. "She might find her way back, and then again, she might not."

Lydia's younger sister, Una, blonde hair and fine white eyelashes. Una had been in the same class at high school as Flora Helsden.

"That one's eyes are full of mischief," Lydia's mother had said when Una brought Flora home.

But Una was the same. No real harm in either of them. Just bubbly girls who'd loved a good laugh, a good time. Lydia turned her head on the pillow, away from the old grief of her sister's death at twenty-two from a rare blood disease. Una and Flora had gone about together, after school and at weekends. Sweetheart necklines on their summer dresses; slender ankles and teetering heels.

A touch at her wrist. Lydia heard Blessica's voice.

"She happy to see you here when she wake up," said the carer.

Who could she be speaking to? Lydia's eyelids felt leaded, yet thoughts came flying in as if winged. Una in a white swimsuit with black polka dots. Something about the swimming baths. Flora in a red bikini. Una and her friend were both sixteen. Una wore goggles because her eyes reacted badly to the chlorine. Flora's brother-in-law had dived in at the deep end and surfaced beside Flora. Swimming underwater, Una had seen the red bikini top pulled down, the brother-in-law with his hands on Flora's breasts. Flora hadn't struggled. Being grabbed underwater, or anywhere, was just something that happened to girls, Una had told Lydia, and Lydia had forgotten all about it. She'd forgotten the name of the brother-in-law, too, until she'd seen those earrings in the newspaper.

Those ugly bite marks in the photographs.

Douglas Clooney, pressing gifts on young Blessica. Still up to his old tricks. Once a sly dog, always a sly dog. He'd been a weak sort of man, like her own son-in-law, Bernard.

Lydia felt the weight of the shadow of the monkey puzzle tree tugging at her eyelids. Close them, then; don't be daunted by disturbing conjunctions. It was an ugly shape for a tree. She should ask to move to a different room.

When Lydia opened her eyes, the shadow had vanished.

"What time is it?"

"It's afternoon tea time," Pixie said, raking coral-coloured nails through her wavy hair.

"I'd like mine with milk and two sugars."

Her daughter looked flushed. She must be anxious.

Lydia said, "I remembered what I wanted to tell you."

"I'll pop out and find someone to make that cuppa," Pixie said.

When Pixie returned with the tea, Lydia was staring out the window at the dark silhouette of the monkey puzzle tree.

Pixie put a mug of tea on the bedside cabinet to cool. "I've filed for divorce," she said. "Living with Bernard has become intolerable."

"Those earrings," Lydia said.

Pixie frowned. "I've been to see Cecil Briggs," she said. "You remember Cecil?"

"Mr Clooney was married to Flora's sister. At the swimming baths …"

"Cecil's confident I'll get the house," Pixie said. "Bernard will have to buy me out."

Blessica came in holding a biscuit tin. "You like biscuit with tea?" she said. "I have coconut ones today."

When Lydia turned from the window her eyes darted from Pixie to Blessica, her expression one of mild confusion.

"What?" she said.

"A biscuit, Mum. She's asking whether you'd like a biscuit."

Lydia turned away towards the window. "Oh! Thank you," she said, "but no."

Blessica smiled and withdrew, and Pixie told Lydia how Bernard had pleaded with her not to leave him.

"He says he'll change," she said. "It seems he likes the status quo."

Lydia's eyes closed. She appeared to have fallen asleep. Pixie gathered up the untouched tea and carried it to the kitchen.

# THE TOWER

With Elizabeth's discovery that she was pregnant, their summer idyll in Brittany crashed to a close. On hearing the news Dorelia had felt a spontaneous rush of joy, but within a heartbeat she realised her mistake. Her friend was trembling, on the edge of tears, while Amos stood with his hands thrust into his pockets, a shocked, sharp look on his face. In the ensuing silence, Dorelia wondered angrily what Amos had expected after all those nights spent drinking and fucking. She had gone out for a walk, leaving them to talk.

In a café, lingering over coffee and Calvados, she had tried to imagine what would happen next. Whatever they decided, Dorelia would return to Sydney. She hadn't the money to remain in France, especially if they no longer had free accommodation on the *Phaedra*. She supposed Elizabeth would go to Manchester with Amos, that there would be a confession, a reconciliation, and a marriage. Respectable girls did not birth children out of wedlock, and although Elizabeth had always been adamant that she would not marry, Dorelia thought it now inevitable. She had tried to assess her own wounds, but beyond a hollowness in the pit of her stomach, she couldn't define her feelings beyond knowing she would mind losing Elizabeth more than losing Amos.

When she returned to the boat, the two had been arguing. Elizabeth snatched up her purse as soon as she sighted Dorelia; her face was blotchy, her movements agitated.

"Come on," she said, "let's find something to eat in town."

Out of habit Dorelia turned to Amos, expecting him to reach for his jacket, pull on his boots and accompany them. Instead, he stared stonily into space, grim and uncommunicative.

Elizabeth took Dorelia's arm and dragged her up the saloon stairs onto the deck.

"Let's get some air," she said, with a backward glance at Amos. "I feel as if I'm being suffocated."

The cafés in the Old Town were opening their doors for the evening, and the narrow streets were already crowded with tourists. They found an empty table at a place they had never eaten at before and from where they could look up at the grey towers and turrets of the Chateau de Saint-Malo.

"Amos asked me to marry him," said Elizabeth.

Dorelia waited, the slender stem of a glass poised between her finger and thumb.

"I told him I would rather die."

"What? But —"

"Amos is going home to work in his father's textile business," Elizabeth said bitterly.

Dorelia sipped her aperitif in silence.

"He'll sit in a dusty office above the factory floor all week, and if his father lets him he'll become a Sunday painter."

"But he's too good for that!"

Elizabeth shrugged. "It's what he deserves," she said, her mouth uncharacteristically hard. "Amos likes nice houses, with plenty of servants; he likes the *Phaedra*, and solid silver cutlery, and gold cufflinks. He likes going to the races, and throwing dinner parties, and has no intention whatsoever of being poor. This summer was only ever an interlude."

"Perhaps you would get used to those things, too," Dorelia said, "if you married him."

Elizabeth leaned across the table, her voice low and harsh. "Are you mad?"

"But the child —"

"Can you imagine me fitting in with those people, his family? And the last thing the Hatherlys want for their precious son is a 'colonial', especially one who fancies herself as an artist."

Dorelia took Elizabeth's hand and squeezed it. "You don't *fancy* yourself as an artist," she said. "You are exquisitely talented; your work is exceptional. Anyone can see."

Elizabeth shook her head. "They would not see. And we would have more children. Who knows how many? It would be the finish of me."

"But if you love Amos …"

"I'd be reduced to a lifetime of hosting charity events, attending church on Sundays and making fatuous social calls. Amos has described how his mother and sisters live, how they expect him and his future wife to live." Elizabeth turned her head and glared up at the castle; she stabbed a finger at one of its turrets. "I'd rather throw myself from that window than give up painting."

# DREAM STREET

Two deaths rocked the town that summer. The first was Dot Letlow's, Dot, who went to bed one night with a headache and in the morning could not be woken. She and her husband Dave lived at the back of The Little Flower Café and Collectables, and when an ambulance had come and gone, and before the doctor and the undertaker arrived, a distraught Dave Letlow staggered through the interconnecting door from their lounge to tape a note in the café window: *Closed until further notice.*

It was a Thursday morning, and Sheena Barry and Kat Tate had just arrived at the café for their waitressing shifts.

"It's locked." Kat rattled the door handle. "What's going on?"

They could see Dave inside, more dishevelled than usual in an old tartan dressing gown over track pants and a T-shirt. The January morning was already warming up, but he was huddled into his clothes as if it were the middle of winter. Kat tapped on the window, but instead of letting them in Dave took down the photograph from the wall above the till.

"What's he doing?" Sheena peered into the darkened cafe.

"Ignoring us," Kat said.

They watched Dave disappear back into the house with the photograph clutched to his chest.

## The Tower

The second death, late in January, was more violent. When news of it broke there were people who said slyly that they were not surprised. Jordan Barry – whose older brother Ryan, it was generally believed, had ended his life some years earlier by crashing his motorbike into a tree – had put a shotgun under his chin. At the inquest it was noted he'd used a short, forked stick to reach the trigger and that his body had lain undiscovered for almost a week.

Jordan had lived alone at a place outside the town known locally as Sitter's Creek. It had been owned decades earlier by an Englishman called Sitter, who had believed he was going to make his fortune digging up silver but instead drank himself to death. His old mine shaft was still there, half filled with smashed beer bottles and other rubbish by tenants and squatters. The land around the house was water-starved and useless, over-run by feral goats, but Jordan had set up a business in one of the outhouses casting plaster garden statues and bird baths. He carved the originals himself, and of the larger figures his Venus and Aphrodite were widely admired, with faces the locals said looked oddly familiar, but couldn't quite identify.

The two garden centres in the town both stocked his statues and not long before he died Jordan had started exporting further afield. A sign propped against the fence at the turnoff to his place read *J. G. Barry, Plaster Art*. Sometimes the wind blew it over, or after a good rain weeds would grow up and obscure it, but there wasn't much passing traffic, and locals who wanted to commission a special piece, or to snap up one of Jordan's seconds, had known where to find him.

It was the solicitor Cecil Briggs who discovered Jordan's body. His wife had asked for a bird bath for her sixtieth and Cecil had been going to commission one with her initials on it, and the date. Instead, he found himself staggering up the hill behind the house in thudding heat, trying to get enough signal on his cell phone to call the police.

"There's a job going for a barmaid at The Rising Sun," Kat said.

She twirled a tendril of red hair that had escaped the scrunchie-held knot on top of her head and tucked it behind an ear. The two girls were smoking under the vine-covered pergola at Kat's mother's place, sifting through the newspaper for jobs.

"Dave's telling people he might open the café again," said Sheena.

"Somehow I can't imagine it, not without Dot."

The two smoked in silence, until Kat said, "That photograph he took off the wall that morning, one of the customers told me it's of their daughter, Rose. She died young, of something awful. Poor Dot! I had no idea."

"That must be why Dot always kept a jam jar of fresh flowers beside it," said Sheena. "If there wasn't anything to pick in their back yard, she'd walk down the street and buy a bunch from the florist."

Kat nodded. "Poor old Dot."

"Little Rose Letlow. I reckon that's why they called the café The Little Flower."

"There's always Coles and Woolies," Kat said. "We could be checkout-chicks."

Sheena pulled a face. "I suppose. If I'm desperate."

"You're still saving to come away, aren't you, Sheen?"

"Course I am. Look, let's aim to go by the beginning of May," said Sheena. "I'll work at the café *and* stack shelves if I have to. I honestly can't take much more of this place."

News of Jordan Barry's death had flown around the town so fast that Freddie Barry's neighbour, Joan Pugsley, had come to the back door with it before anyone in their family had rung to break it to them. Sheena had found Joan hovering on the kitchen step and smiled at the woman to mask her dislike.

"Mrs Pugsley! Mum's just round the side, watering."

In Joan Pugsley's pudding face, her currant eyes shone with suppressed excitement.

"You'd better ask her to step inside, dear."

The news of her uncle's death brought up all Sheena's unease around her father's motorbike accident. And then there was her mother Freddie, looking as if someone had suddenly switched off all her lights.

"This is going to kill Gran Barry," Sheena said, when they'd finally managed to get rid of Joan Pugsley.

She waited for her mother to say they would have to go and see her Gran, but Freddie just sat at the kitchen table with her hands wrapped around a mug of cooling coffee and did not reply. Sheena raked her fingers through her pale pink hair in which the roots were showing; there was a darkness in the house that made her long to fling open all the doors and windows, or to run outside and keep on running. She had long suspected something between her mother and Jordan Barry, but shied away from thinking about it.

Luckily, Jesse came in then. Her brother was better at dealing with their mother than she was, and sure enough, instead of saying anything he went straight to her and put his arms around her. This seemed to draw some life back into Freddie.

"You heard, then?" she said.

"Yeah. I'll walk round and pick up Benny from day care," Jesse said.

"Will you?"

"Yeah. You put your feet up."

The news about Jordan had wiped Benny from Sheena's mind, but not from Jesse's. Now she wondered why she hadn't offered to pick up her little brother, when her mother was sitting there looking gutted. Sheena tugged at the ends of her hair. She was truly useless when it came to comforting anyone. Maybe there was something wrong with her, because she never knew what to say or do when people were hurting – she had learned that about herself when her father died.

# Dream Street

It was late night shopping, and while Jesse went to get Benny, Sheena decided to walk into town and buy a treat for her mother. There was that little place that had opened in the old arcade, and Freddie had bought a few things home from there – packets of incense and scented candles, even a dress in thin Indian cotton. The shop sold healing crystals, and if anyone could do with a healing crystal or a scented candle right now, it was her mother. Sheena brushed her hair, put on fresh lipstick, and set off.

There was the usual bustle in the main street, cars driving up and down, most of them boys with their P plates showing off to each other. When she and Kat were at high school this broad dusty street with its verandah-shaded shopfronts had been the centre of their universe, although they had never called it by its name, it was always just The Street. Let's go up The Street after school, she or Kat would say, and it had been something to look forward to through dull afternoons of algebra, and history, and English composition.

It was dusk, and the temperature had dropped a little, although heat still radiated from the pavements and from the old stone shop fronts. Sheena passed W. J. Horrocks's empty butcher's shop with its flaking sign; it had been forced out of businesss half a decade earlier by the two new supermarkets. Her mother used to send her there to buy sausages, and slices of cold corned beef or devon. Sheena remembered the shop's meaty smell, and how the sawdust on the floor worked its way into her sandals as she waited for old Bill Horrocks to wrap her order.

On past the greengrocer's and the dusty little store that sold Akubra hats and riding boots to the tourists. At the corner, the bronze soldier in battle-dress loomed against the evening sky. A few dessicated wreaths were propped at the foot of the war memorial's granite plinth. Further on past the town hall was Prouds the jewellers. In the late afternoons, schoolgirls clustered outside its brightly lit windows, giggling and pointing;

on Saturday mornings young women out shopping stopped to browse the displays. Sometimes there were couples looking at engagement rings – often the men appeared uneasy, as if they'd been dragged there against their will. But it was the female faces that troubled Sheena most, the naked yearning they forgot to disguise, as they gazed at the velvet pads studded with diamond rings.

From their first years of high school, most of the girls she knew had been dreaming of the day a man would surprise them by producing one of Prouds white satin-lined ring boxes from his coat pocket. But between the stammered proposal of a beau and their first imagining of him, lay years of walking up The Street on hot afternoons to stare into those windows, either with a group of friends, or furtively alone. Sheena thought that if she could photograph girls' faces as they stood with their noses pressed to the glass, their outer shells would dissolve and all that would show on film would be lumps of pure, throbbing, heart-shaped ambition.

Her mother's engagement and wedding rings had come from Prouds. Freddie had often teased Ryan about how long it had taken him to get her engagement ring off lay-by.

"That's because it was nearly the biggest bloody rock in the shop," he'd say. "I could have bought a small house for what that ring cost."

Freddie would thrust out her left hand and wriggle her fingers until the diamonds flashed pink and blue and yellow fire.

"Worth every penny," she'd say. "Plus if we fall on hard times we can always sell it."

"If times get that bloody hard, who'll buy it?" Ryan would shoot back.

Freddie had laughed. While they were paying off the house they'd never had much money, but neither of them had seriously imagined a time when they might have to flog Freddie's ring to pay the bills.

At some point their laughing and teasing had stopped, and it wouldn't be fair to say it was the strain of raising Benny. Sheena had been fourteen when Benny was born, sixteen by the time they knew he had a problem and started pursuing a diagnosis. No, the laughter had petered out of her parents' marriage before Benny was born. As a baby, Jesse was never a good sleeper, so her mother was often scratchy and the house was always messy with his toys. Her father had started drinking more heavily. Maybe that had been at the root of it. Whenever Sheena thought of him he was sitting in his old recliner listening to a horse race on the radio, a long neck of West End Draught in his hand and another one empty on the floor beside him.

She'd long ago decided marriage was a mistaken aspiration. It started as a dream and ended as a nightmare. Who would give up their entire being, to become absorbed into the life of some young dimwitted bloke like those hooning up and down The Street? Someone who within a few years would have a beer belly and be down the betting shop every night, while the wife stayed at home and raised the kids? Sheena had watched this happen to her mother, and it was beginning to happen to the young women she and Kat had gone to school with. Despite encouragement from the Careers Advisor, most girls she knew still dreamed of a white wedding, a husband and kids. Feminism had made little headway, other than to make them think they could drink like young men did when they went out partying. Yet years ago, maybe even on one of those excursions down The Street to linger over nut sundaes in the Astoria milk bar, she and Kat had made a solemn pact that there were to be no engagements, no serious boyfriends before they'd given their single lives a bloody good shake.

Sure enough, there were window-shoppers outside Prouds, young faces staring in greedily at the goods. The boys hanging about on the pavement all had their backs to the windows; they were watching The Street, and something about them reminded Sheena of her father watering the front lawn in shorts and bare feet while keeping one eye on anyone passing along Knox Street. When he was feeling playful he would hold the spray high while she, and later Jesse, did cartwheels through it.

Sheena hadn't thought about her father like this in a long while. She leaned against a darkened shop window, a hand to her chest, and in the glow of tail-lights up The Street and the sudden *doof doof* from a car with its windows down, she saw her parents dancing in their kitchen – the flick of Freddie's skirt as their dad twirled her under his arm, and the two of them fell together, laughing. Where had those times gone? Had they even been real? All the afternoon barbecues with the backyard full of kids, the cricket bats and home-made stumps, the shopping trips where he'd push them in the trolley, the birthday cakes and candles, all the small rituals of family life that had seemed to hold them together, but in the end hadn't been strong enough.

Sheena eyed the window-shoppers with dismay and then with a sharp intake of breath. One of them was Kat Tate, and beside her stood the young policeman Kat had always said had no chance in hell with her, not a single one. They were so absorbed in whatever they were staring at in the window that they hadn't noticed Sheena.

"Why didn't you tell me you were serious about Ted Capelli?"

Kat shrugged. "I don't know. I kept hoping the feeling would wear off."

"But it hasn't?"

Kat lit a cigarette and stared moodily at its smouldering tip. "I don't know."

"Well, the two of you were looking at engagement rings."

"What, are you spying on me now?"

"I was down The Street to pick up something for Mum."

Kat flicked ash, an impatient movment. "Going there was Ted's idea. Maybe I am in love with him, maybe I'm not. I suppose time will tell."

"Well, are you still coming to Adelaide?"

Kat hesitated, and Sheena exploded. "So you're going to ditch the plans we've had since forever, to become Mrs Capelli! We promised to talk each other out of falling into that old trap. Remember?"

"I know. Look, Sheen, I'm still coming, all right? It'll help me sort my feelings, if I'm away from him for a while."

But there was something different about Kat, a sleekness that suggested she was lapping up Ted's adoration, whereas for a long time it had left her unmoved. Sheena had seen the way Ted Capelli looked at Kat as they stood together outside the jeweller's shop, and sensed that getting her away from him was to be a battle she mightn't win.

"Well, Dave rang to say he's reopening the café," Sheena said. "We can have our old jobs back, if you're interested."

Sheena and Kat had gone together to Dot's funeral. They'd stood and wept into their handkerchiefs as the coffin was lowered, and afterwards, on the way back to the car, they'd taken a detour to visit the grave of Kat's ancestor who'd been murdered, seventeen-year-old Flora Helsden. The grave was marked by a white marble cross, and the girls were familiar with it, having gone together to leave flowers on the anniversary of Flora's death. Now they were shocked to see that vandals had wrenched the cross from its base and that some of the marble roses from the wreath that encircled it had been broken away.

"Who'd do this?" Kat stared aghast at the destruction.

Wordlessly, Sheena pointed at the slab where Flora's name and date of death were inscribed and on which someone with a spray can had scrawled *Whore!* in red metallic paint.

"But it was years ago, why would anyone do this now?" Kat's voice rasped out of her, as if she'd been running.

"You'd think it was random, if it wasn't for that paint," Sheena said.

"Exactly! Someone in this town's still got a stake in what happened to Flora."

Sheena knelt and gathered the fragments of the roses into a neat pile. When Dot was still alive, Sheena had been sorting vintage jewellery for the collectables side of the café's business when a pair of earrings had turned up that were like the ones Flora had worn on the night she was murdered. It was thought the murderer had taken them for a souvenir, and suddenly there they were, decades later, at the bottom of a cardboard box full of items from the local auction mart. Dot had rung the police to report the find, and Ted Capelli had come and taken the earrings away to the station.

"Did Ted ever say what happened after we handed in those earrings?" Sheena said. "The ones that looked like Flora's."

"He said they were investigating. But that was months ago."

Sheena wanted to spit that Kat ought to ask Ted about it next time he took her window-shopping at Prouds, but as they started back to the car she stayed silent.

"I'll ask him again," Kat said dully. "Mum will want to get this gravestone mended. She'll be furious at the expense."

"Dave's been acting weird. Have you noticed?" Kat said.

"It's not long since Dot's funeral," said Sheena.

"But still. He was wearing one of her cardigans yesterday," Kat said. "The grey one that's gone a bit pilled."

"It's only a cardigan. Maybe now Dot's not here to sort out the washing, Dave doesn't realise it's hers."

Kat looked sceptical. "Well, I think it's a bit creepy." A customer came in then and she dropped the subject. But later, as they were clearing up before closing, she whispered to Sheena that it wasn't just the grey cardigan.

"That shirt Dave's got on, that was Dot's."

Sheena shrugged. Dot would have been horrified, but she would never know, and they would soon be away from all this.

Kat slipped her arms out of the pale green overall that was their uniform at The Little Flower.

"I asked Ted about those earrings and at first he said he couldn't say anything."

"But?"

Kat lowered her voice. "They've disappeared from the police file."

"The police have lost them?"

"That's what he said." Kat picked up her handbag. "I told him about the vandalism at Flora's grave, the graffitti. He reckons it happens all the time, but I don't know, it feels like this whole town is conspiring to cover up what happened to Flora."

The sleekness had drained from Kat's face and from her sturdy body. To Sheena she looked stronger, more like her old indomitable self.

"Listen, Sheen," Kat said, as they let themselves out of the cafe and pulled the door shut behind them, "Let's not wait until May. Let's go right now. I know you wanted to take more cash, but we'll manage somehow."

"Now?"

"Tonight. Mum's bought a new car and she's given me her old one." Kat grinned. "We could pack a few things and jump in it and go."

"Seriously?"

Kat laughed. "Yeah! After all, if it doesn't work out we can always come back."

"Well ..." A small voice in Sheena's head whispered that it was only ever a one-way ticket, that was the only ticket you could buy when you chose to leave home. But she was shivering with excitement.

## The Tower

"Are you sure? What about you and Ted?"

Kat's eyes narrowed. "Ted's the reason I'm sure," she said. "Let's get out, Sheen, let's get away from here, before we can't."

# THE TOWER

They had sailed the *Phaedra* from St Malo to Jersey, Amos having picked up a young Spaniard to crew for him. Neither Dorelia nor Elizabeth had any experience of sailing, but in any case they were disabled by seasickness and spent the first part of the voyage sweating out their nausea in the forward cabin. From Jersey they crossed the English Channel to Southampton, then along the coast, port-hopping, until they anchored in Rye Harbour. Amos had an aunt there who he said would help them.

Eviane Bell's guest house was perched on the edge of the ancient town of Rye. They had arrived on a dark and windy September afternoon, and as both the women had soaked their shoes disembarking from the *Phaedra*, they had taken them off and appeared at Eviane's front door with bare feet. She showed no surprise, but ushered them into a lounge, where an elderly black whippet lying in front of the fire stood up and came forward to greet them. There were brown birds on the wallpaper and soft light from small table lamps; the curtains were drawn against the autumn chill, and Eviane herself brought them glasses of sherry. She was, they would soon discover, a true bohemian, and when Elizabeth expressed her surprise, Amos admitted that his aunt was regarded as the black sheep of the family.

With her dark waving hair bundled up with red-lacquer clasps and a face like a pre-Raphaelite angel who had chosen to age like a human rather than remain eternally young, Eviane was also practical and energetic, and immensely kind.

"Luckily, it's coming up to the off-season," she said. "I always invite a few artists to spend the winter here because their body heat keeps the damp out of the wallpaper." She offered them her radiant smile. "You're the first to arrive, so you can have your pick of the rooms."

They chose two attic bedrooms from which they could look out across the narrow river to the town, and Amos explained to his aunt that Elizabeth would wait out her pregnancy here. This revelation was greeted by an accepting shrug from Eviane. Amos would return to Manchester to arrange a private adoption.

With Amos gone, Dorelia and Elizabeth had unpacked their paints. When the weather was poor they took turns sitting for each other indoors, but whenever it was fine enough to go out they painted in odd corners of the town, capturing its cobbled streets and narrow houses in dozens of small studies. Until Elizabeth's condition made expeditions further afield impractical, they would often set off into the surrounding countryside, tramping for miles around the edges of fields and on public footpaths. The two of them together outdoors, painting side by side, each critiquing the other's work – this was how Dorelia had imagined their time in France would be spent, before Amos had inserted himself into the picture.

Now that he was no longer with them, the spell he had cast over her had evaporated. Dorelia accepted she had never loved Amos; it had been at best an infatuation. Which was a relief, because she had avoided a broken heart. For Elizabeth, it was different, because of course she was carrying Amos's child. That the conception had been a mistake did not alter the baby's existence, and whether Elizabeth would be able to part with it when the time came still remained to be seen. And yet it was unthinkable that she would take the baby back to Australia. Her parents might not throw her out on the street, she said, but they would make sure she paid dearly for her mistake. For Elizabeth the choice was not between giving up the child or keeping it, it was between becoming a mother and continuing as an artist.

In the final weeks before the birth, Elizabeth grew steadily more silent. Dorelia imagined the struggle that was going on in her friend's mind, for by now the baby was moving, it was real; with a hand on Elizabeth's swollen stomach, even Dorelia had felt its healthy kick. Strangely, in this time in Rye, Elizabeth's painting had taken a forward leap. It was as if everything she had seen and learned in France had been distilled and then set aside, as she focused on mastering ever-finer gradations of grey. The paintings she made were all keyed to a grey, white, and black colour scheme, with touches of ochre and umber, and tiny flame-like flashes of crimson, or teal. It was the period in which she developed the tonal palette she would work with for years to come, ignoring art movements and changing fashions.

Eviane insisted Elizabeth must paint her portrait, and she had been working on it when she went into labour. The baby was born in the attic, sucking in with her first breath the fumes of oil paint, of linseed oil, and turps, to the undisguised dismay of the midwife.

# PLUNGES

"Linden? Lin? Can you hear me, Mrs Ledwidge?"

Surely that is her mother's voice, floating above her in the darkness. That fuzziness at the edges of words Moira gets after the first couple of gins. Her mother is calling up the stairwell, begging Linden to come down. From the sound of her, she is well into that unopened bottle that was on the sideboard after school. But Linden isn't coming down. No way. The darkness is soothing.

"Just squeeze my hand if you can hear me, Linden dear."

Not her mother, then. Moira's touch was never that firm. Linden is aware of a light being shone into her eyes, a torch, is it? A nurse with a green cap and gown hovers over her, a young face, scattered with freckles. Despite wanting only to plunge back into the warm, breathy darkness from which this nurse's voice has summoned her, Linden gathers her strength and squeezes. The hand gripping hers squeezes back, and a second nurse brings a baby close to her face.

"Here he is," she says, "the little treasure."

He is tightly wrapped in a white blanket. Linden sees his tiny blue-rimmed mouth, as round as the letter 'O'.

"A beautiful boy," the first voice says. "We'll have you sitting up and holding him in a little while."

But Linden doesn't want to sit up. She doesn't want to hold this baby they are showing her. Why are they tormenting her with someone's newborn, when she has just been through some kind of crisis?

Light flares through the gauzy curtains in the room they have wheeled her to after the operating theatre and the recovery room. There are flowers everywhere, stiff florist's arrangements that ought to be pulled apart and the wires removed. Charlie is there, smiling at her with tears in his eyes. What on earth does he have to cry about?

The worst thing is that they won't let her sleep. All she wants is darkness and silence, but they keep waking her and pressing that infant to her breast. Why can't someone else feed it? Why does it have to be her?

They are careful never to leave her alone with the baby. She notices that. Someone must have told them what it was like after the others were born. What are their names? Linden lies with her eyes closed, struggling to think. Josh. Caitlin. Of course, they are hers and Charlie's children. She had the breakdown after Josh, and Caitlin wasn't easy. She needn't go through with it a third time, the doctor had said, offering termination. But she'd had to, of course, because the guilt would have haunted her to the end of time.

If only they would let her sleep. If only this tiny creature were not so voracious for her milk. How long is the rest of her life going to be? Linden wants darkness and silence.

"Time for his next feed, Mrs Ledwidge."

Now she's started thinking about her mother, she can't stop. Moira waving to her from an upstairs window when they had first moved to the house on the Isle of Man. She had been cheerful at first because there were blinds and curtains to be ordered, a new kitchen to install. Minor repairs and alterations meant the coming and going of tradesmen, so weekdays had busyness and purpose. Then at weekends her father was with them. Linden's school routine had been another steadying influence. Each school morning after breakfast she'd left the house and walked the short distance to the cross roads to board the Castletown bus. That was when her mother would wave to her from an upstairs window, and as the bus pulled away there'd be the flutter of her handkerchief.

God knows what Moira did with the rest of her day if there were no workmen to make tea for. Probably those were the mornings when she drove to the bottle shop in Castletown. One afternoon after school, when her mother had been too drunk to drive, she'd pleaded with Linden to walk into town and pick up something for her, a tipple to ward off the cold she was brewing. The man behind the counter had smiled at Linden when she entered the bottle shop, and before she'd even asked for anything he'd slipped a bottle of Gordon's gin into a brown paper bag and handed it to her.

"I'll put it on the account," he'd said, not meeting her eye.

She'd been speechless with shame. They had only been on the island a month.

School mornings, and the builders, had kept Moira more or less on an even keel at the beginning. But even then, coming home in the afternoons, a heaviness had crept over Linden as soon as she sighted the grey silhouette of their house from the bus. If a tradie's van were parked out the front, everything inside might be all right. Or if there were a twist of smoke rising from the chimney – Moira only lit the fire when she was feeling good. If there were no workman's van, Linden would slide her key into the front door and open it silently.

Her father said they had moved to the Isle of Man to maximise his financial position, but Linden thought it was because of her mother, the trouble there'd been at their old place.

In Manchester, Moira had avoided a conviction for drunk and disorderly by agreeing to a stint in a sanatorium. A rest cure, she'd called it, and when she came out, they had packed up and gone to live on the island.

The move meant her father could look forward to an early retirement, he said. Linden longed for him to be at home all the time, but he was an airline pilot and she was sad that he would have to give up flying. It was the only thing he'd ever wanted to do with his life, that and to marry her mother. Why would he have wanted Moira? Linden had never been able to come up with a satisfactory answer, although when her mother put on a fresh dress and took trouble with her hair, when she hadn't yet poured the first drink of the evening, even Linden could see that Moira really might once have been, as she insisted when drunk, 'the most beautiful woman in Hartlepoole'.

They were not in the least alike, as Moira sometimes pointed out with a viciousness that baffled Linden. Her fine-boned mother was bird-like, with pale hair waved close against her tiny head like one of the old black-and-white movie stars, whereas she was long-limbed, dark-eyed and dark-haired, and set to grow even taller than her father. And not only were they physically different, but they had never achieved the closeness Linden saw in other mothers and daughters. She put it down to the effects of alcohol and accepted that she would always be what Moira referred to bitterly as a Daddy's Girl.

They are taking the baby home. He is theirs, Charlie insists, even though Linden feels he might be anyone's.

"Are you sure?" She had whispered to the nurses who had brought him to her to be fed. "Are you sure this one is mine?"

They had smiled, as if she'd made a joke.

"Of course! This is little Louis. Look, here's his name on his wristband."

What Linden thinks is that anyone could have slipped that wristband over his tiny hand. Who would know? All the babies look more or less the same, though some have more hair. The thing she can't deny is that one of them belongs to her. They have cut open her body and extracted a baby. And now she and Charlie have brought a baby home – her own, or one of the others.

Charlie's mother has flown out from England to help.

The school on the island was a grey stone fortress with a distinctive clock tower. It was so close to Ronaldsway airport that Linden could watch for the planes that brought her father home on Friday afternoons and took him away again on Sundays. She was at school on Sundays because towards the end of that first term her father had explained that she would have to become a boarder.

"You see how things are with your mother," he said. "I'll feel happier going back across if I know you're safe at school. At least until things calm down."

The first friend Linden made among the boarders was Dilys Pringle. Dilys, too, had started that term. It was not only their new and daunting surroundings that drew the two together, but the similarity of their situations, for they both had absent fathers and what Dilys described as 'a mother problem'.

Now Linden has become the problem mother. It is a sad irony. Charlie says not to be morbid, not to take everything to heart. They have three beautiful children, the family they always wanted. But Linden wonders now whether she ever did want three children. She and Charlie must have discussed it, but she can't remember.

Charlie had arrived in Linden's second year at boarding school. He'd been sent there because his father had been a boarder, as had his grandfather. Matthew and William Ledwidge: their names were up in gold on the old scholars' board in the assembly hall. After Dilys's parents got back together their family had moved to Ireland, and Charlie had become Linden's best friend. Their house masters kept a close eye on them. But despite their surveillance, in their final year they had found the abandoned store-room off one of the landings in the clock tower. It had been dark in that windowless room, which was perfect, because they were so young and inexpert, and Linden, at least, was self-conscious about her body.

They had emerged as different people – radiant, no longer obsessed about small imperfections. They would always be perfect together, Charlie had said.

Linden tries to recall when being a couple was no longer enough for Charlie. When was it he had decided he wanted a family, children, someone other than her? She must have agreed. She must have. And here they are now, all five of them, on the edge of something.

Charlie's mother sits in their bright white living-room, some old, dark grief pooled inside her like a lake deep within a cave. She is a quiet woman, yet her presence is not restful. Linden ponders why this should be and decides that her mother-in-law is not so much quiet as watchful. It is being watched that gets on Linden's nerves. When she mentions this to Charlie, he tries not to let her see that he is offended, but he is, of course.

"Don't look for trouble where there is none," he says. "Mum is solid. She's here to help."

The plane on the flight her father was to pilot to North Africa was a Boeing 737. There were one-hundred-and-thirty-nine passengers and six crew on board when it caught fire during take-off and plunged onto the runway. As the plane came to a halt, fire warnings sounded in the flight deck. Evacuation was ordered, but one of the front exit doors jammed. Panicked passengers then clogged the other exits. While fire engines sprayed them with foam, the rear door was opened, whereupon a westerly breeze carried dense smoke and flames into the passenger compartment. Survivors reported that the aisle had been blocked with bodies. Fifty-nine passengers and four crew perished, including Linden's father. Most of them died from inhaling toxic smoke.

Strange, the details that stick in the mind, like the wallpaper in the kitchen of that grey house on the island. Bunches of red cherries on a white background; Moira chose it, just as she chose the scarlet work surfaces and the dark wooden cupboards. So much red. Her father's unguarded razor in the bathroom. If Linden had been living at home these things might have alerted her to what would happen when her mother plunged deeper into the bottle. Somehow Moira had survived, to be spirited away to Ballamona, the psychiatric hospital.

Afterwards, Linden had wanted to stay at boarding school. It was the only safe place she knew. She and Charlie had married young and he'd brought her to live in Canada. They were to leave the past behind them, he had said, but Linden had carried it with her.

The nurse who does the home visits wants Linden to switch to bottle-feeds. It will allow someone else to take over at night, so that she can rest. But breast milk gives babies the best start. This was drummed into them at the pre-natal classes when Linden was expecting Josh and again with Caitlin. She'll manage the night feeds a while longer, she says, even though her mother-in-law is itching to help.

"I don't sleep," she says, "so I might as well be warming a bottle."

But Linden shakes her head. "Not yet," she says, her voice firm. Out of the corner of her eye she sees Charlie's eye-roll and his mother's slight shrug, and fury bubbles in her throat. Why is Charlie taking his mother's side?

## The Tower

After the final feed of the night, with the baby asleep in her arms, Linden plucks the car keys from the wall-hook in the kitchen. There is a picnic spot she and Charlie used to go to when Josh was tiny. You couldn't take children there once they could walk, or you'd be forever shouting at them to keep away from the edge. Far below the cliffs was a lake, a shining expanse of dark water, like a lake in a dream.

The cold pre-dawn light is a dense porous grey, with the faintest tinge of pink over the distant treetops. Linden clips the baby into the harness in his travel cot in the car's back seat and reverses out onto the road.

As the eastern sky lightens, the trees and houses slipping by on either side huddle motionless and dark. Soon there are fewer houses, and then a sprinkling, and then none. Mist rises in her headlights. It's not far now to the picnic spot – there's a winding climb and then the road flattens out. She sees that the sky is still pricked with stars, though they are dimming.

With the heater on, the car is warming at last. She parks in the place where they always parked – closer to the edge than she'd thought was safe, but Charlie had never had her problem with heights. Linden unclips the baby and sits in the front passenger seat with him in her lap. His tiny chest rises and falls so lightly that sometimes she's uncertain if he's actually breathing.

She wonders where Dilys is now and whether she ever married and had children. Once she'd met Charlie, she'd lost touch with Dilys. It had been her fault, because the letters had kept coming from Ireland, until Linden had gradually stopped answering. It's shameful, the way women drop their friends as soon as they're in a romantic relationship. But Charlie had been the same with his mates. They'd been enough for each other.

There is a pack of Charlie's cigarettes in the space between the seats. Linden lights one and opens the window a few inches to exhale the smoke. She sees the red and white kitchen, and her father there bent over the washing up, sleeves rolled up to his elbows and a tea towel on his shoulder. It is his kindness she remembers. Had he lived, he would have been forever tormented by those deaths.

So often, she has closed her eyes and imagined the final take-off. And then the explosion and the plunging descent. She has imagined the terror of the passengers strapped into their seats and the struggle in the cockpit. It must be all of this, she thinks, that played over in her mother's mind, replacing whatever personal terrors that once filled her and only abated when she'd had enough to drink. But they would not have allowed her to drink in that place where she was an inmate for years. For Moira's sake, Linden hopes they had other methods of exorcising terror, though she doubts that they did.

She throws the cigarette out of the window: her baby must not inhale smoke. He opens his eyes then and for the first time she is transfixed by his piercing, sapphire gaze. The look he offers her is defenceless, so sweet and deep; it might be the secret entrance to a bottomless lake. Linden strokes his cheek.

"Hello, wee treasure."

She draws a long slow breath and plunges deep.

# THE TOWER

It was often so warm in the tower that Dorelia's eyes would begin to droop even before she'd eaten her midday sandwich. She carried up a portable fan and set it on the bookcase, but the steady hum of its blades, and the wafted air, only increased her sense that she was afloat on a stretch of calm water. The wing chair, with the ottoman pulled close, was as comfortable as a daybed. Unlike her restless nights downstairs, when Dorelia slept in the tower she fell into a deep and dreamless state that left her refreshed on waking, if a little dazed. And not only dazed, but guilty for the wasted time. Time was the one thing she was short of, and not only days and weeks, or if she were lucky, years, but the precious days and weeks and years in which she still had her faculties, and her freedom.

There had been occasional tiny slips into a place Dorelia had no words for; it was like stepping out of your own front door and finding yourself in an unfamiliar street. The first time it happened was in the old house, a couple of days after Geordie's funeral. She had just come out of the shower and was reaching for a towel, when she happened to find herself staring into the bathroom mirror. It was a thing she usually avoided, because the sight of her scrawny frame with its wrinkled and spotted upholstery reminded her that she was far older than she felt.

## The Tower

Not that she minded being old – after all, there was nothing to be done about it. What she resented was that the deterioration of the human body had to be so unattractive.

Anyway, there she was, still slippery from the shower, and in the mirror she saw a woman staring out at her with huge, dark, frightened eyes. Time had seemed to pause as they regarded each other across the sink. Who was this old woman with her damp grey hair pinned on top of her head? Why was she standing there with her bottom lip trembling and her eyes welling up? Dorelia's mind had turned sluggish, but eventually a thought had come: Oh yes, I know, it's that woman who's just buried her husband, poor thing. She'd returned to the present moment with a little jump, as when you fall asleep and then wake again, and a not unreasonable reluctance to think about what had just happened. Since then, there had been other slips. They never lasted long, but the confusion they caused could linger for days. They were a secret worry that gnawed at her, one she hadn't confided even to Bunty.

Yet overall, a deep sense of wellbeing engulfed Dorelia in the tower. She knew it was as important to embrace the restorative naps as to push on with her writing, that time spent resting was not really time wasted.

She had submitted 'Rapunzel's Witch' to an anthology of stories about older women, and when it was accepted, she and Bunty opened a bottle of bubbles.

"Who is to be next?" Bunty asked.

The wicked stepmother in *Snow White* was on Dorelia's radar, though on re-reading the story she thought perhaps that woman was beyond anyone's power to redeem. As well as the fairy tales, her list included characters from classic literature, and one or two – like Mrs Appleyard the headmistress from Joan Lindsay's *Picnic at Hanging Rock*, and the housekeeper Mrs Danvers from *Rebecca* – were from more recent fiction. Bunty urged her to consider Lady Macbeth. The trouble was that the stories all hinged on these old women behaving badly. To turn it around for them you had to read against the narrative grain. It was exhausting, yet this was the work she had chosen; it was a mental limbering up, before she settled back into her memoir.

One afternoon, sunk in delicious slumber, Dorelia became dimly aware of a tapping at one of the windows. Still swimming a gentle breaststroke through warm streams of sleep, her eyes flicked open to see a face staring in through one of the windows, its mouth moving soundlessly against the glass. Propelled by shock from her chair, Dorelia tripped on the flex from the fan and fell, clipping the corner of the bookcase with her right temple.

There was a shriek from outside, but Dorelia paid it no attention. Somehow, she disentangled her legs from the electrical flex and sat up, holding her head. The face at the window had vanished and now there was shouting and banging downstairs. Lurching and dizzy, Dorelia made her way down, one hand on the banister rail and the other clasping her throbbing temple. She opened the front door just as her youngest daughter shattered the stained-glass side panel with a brick.

"What on earth are you doing!"

"Mummy, you're *bleeding*!" Gwenyth was weeping, and Mel was on her mobile phone calling an ambulance.

Dorelia, shoes crunching over broken glass, protested. "I don't need an ambulance."

But there was blood streaming down her neck and soaking her blouse. She remembered the blood thinners she took, and that she was supposed to be careful if she cut herself. Perhaps, after all, she ought to go to hospital.

# YES, NO, MAYBE SO

"Tell the truth, Benny, am I too old to be wearing pink hair?"

Sheena Barry squeezed her brother's hand, but Benny wouldn't make eye contact. They were sitting on the floor in front of a puzzle in which flat pieces could be fitted into frames to form highly coloured fruits. Sheena had been there an hour, and after making a start Benny had pushed the puzzle away, though for once not violently. He'd been staring at his socked feet ever since, intent on wriggling his toes in a kind of Mexican wave.

When he was a child Benny had played with Lego. He'd never actually constructed anything, but fiddling with the pieces was the only calm activity he had seemed to enjoy. Sheena wished she could bring him some Lego, but it was banned from the care home. She'd asked a couple of times, explaining that it stimulated Benny, but the answer was always a head shake. Residents might shove pieces into their mouths; they could choke to death on a block of Lego. Fair enough, but it was tough on her brother.

"I guess the jury is still out on pink hair," Sheena said.

She released Benny's hand, then stood up and reached for her handbag. The big glass doors reflected her slender figure in a vintage dress, and the pink, blunt-cut bob. Sheena raised her chin: maybe at thirty she really was still rocking the pink hair. Once, her friend Kat Tate would have given her an honest answer about it, but Kat was back in the city and for the last few years their catch-ups had been few and far between.

"Bye, Bens, until next time."

Sheena stooped and kissed the top of her brother's head, and the tawny hair against her mouth, its coarse texture, had a faintly sour smell. When he didn't look up, she walked to the door that led to reception and waited to be buzzed out.

On the corner along from Benny's care home was a new McDonald's, the line of cars in its drive-through a sign of the way the town had changed. Once, there had only been the Astoria Milk Bar, Giorgio's Coffee Lounge, a few greasy spoon places, and The Little Flower Café and Collectables, where Sheena and Kat had worked. Now, as well as the fast-food franchises, there were half-a-dozen restaurants, and of the private galleries still in business, one or two had expanded to include cafes. A few years back, with jobs dwindling in the mines, blokes who had never painted in their lives had picked up brushes and tubes of oil paint and gone out into the bush to reinvent themselves as artists. They'd built exhibition spaces onto their houses, where they sold the originals alongside signed prints and bush-art-themed souvenirs. Sheena had thought their paintings crude, but unlikely as it seemed, the galleries had flourished; tourists still couldn't get enough of their work.

She had come back to the town to help her mother empty their old house in Knox Street and ready it for sale. Freddie needed the money for Benny's residential care and for the alternative therapies she still insisted on trying for him. In the past it had been acupuncture, and therapeutic art; more lately there had been strange diets, and something called bio-resonance. None of it had made a difference to Benny. Once the house was sold, Freddie would move into a granny flat in her brother Don's back yard. Sheena was on her way there to measure the windows for new curtains.

It was late afternoon, and the outback light was syrupy, gilding tin and wooden houses, soaking the broad, empty streets of the town in a temporary sweetness. It was a light filmmakers would wait all week for. Sheena thought then of Seb Parish, saw him pulling a lump of molten glass from the furnace and spinning it on the end of his blow pipe, using his breath to bring out some beautiful and useful shape – a fruit bowl streaked with swirling colours, or a small glass animal to delight a child. Seb Parish, who wanted to marry her.

Sheena had tried to explain why she was so resistant to becoming a wife.

"Even if a marriage works, there'll come a day when a wife will wake up middle-aged, a mere housekeeper, to find that her husband is no longer excited by loving her and the children are leaving home. Then what will there be for her to look forward to? What will be left of the person she once was?"

Seb had listened without interrupting, and when she had finished, he'd shaken his head.

"Maybe that might have been true once, Sheena," he said, "but this isn't the dark ages."

The worst of it was that she wanted to believe him.

When Sheena and Kat had first moved to Adelaide, they had shared a room in a B&B in Parkside. After a week of scouring the situations vacant, Kat had scooped a live-in position as a child-minder and general dogsbody in an enormous old house in North Adelaide. Left alone in the B&B, knowing no one, Sheena had hoped it would be her turn soon, because the buzz of the city wasn't so thrilling when you were on your own.

With her savings dwindling, she had accepted a job in a dress shop in one of the city's dowdier arcades. It had been a relief to have money coming in rather than trickling away. Her boss, Tania, was opening a second, smaller store specialising in cocktail-wear, and if Sheena could sell, Tania promised, she'd be put in charge.

In the mornings, polishing the shop's plate glass windows with methylated spirits and a wad of newspaper, Sheena had tried not to wonder what was happening at home – she was on the brink of a bright new life, and it didn't do to look back. But the promised stewardship of the cocktail-wear shop had never eventuated. Tania installed one of her cousins as manager, and Sheena remained as an assistant at the original store. There on weekdays, and half days on Saturdays, wilting for lack of natural light, she had watched her boss flatter customers and lie about what suited them; anything was fair, as long as it culminated in a sale. Half the garments Tania pressed on those hapless women were so unsuitable that Sheena guessed they would languish unworn in wardrobes, their price tags furtively concealed from husbands. Sheena preferred to find clothes that both flattered a customer's figure and made them feel comfortable, so that maybe they'd come back and buy something else. But Tania scolded when she offered too much choice.

"It's a case of which garments we want to shift," she said, "never mind trying everything on the racks!"

One day, Sheena watched her boss pushing a yellow linen pant suit on an elderly and rather elegant woman. The colour was hideous against her ageing skin, and the jacket was six inches too long, which made her look short and dowdy. When Tania was called to the telephone, Sheena had gone to the fitting room holding a grey wool dress with white trim.

"Excuse me," she'd said, "but I think this is perfect for you. Would you like to try it on?"

The elderly woman had been Simone Bagot-Black, owner of Bagot-Black Fine Art. When she'd paid for the grey dress, she had slipped her card into Sheena's hand.

"Ring me," she'd whispered.

Sheena had gone to work for Simone as her personal assistant. They had laughed over the yellow pant suit.

"I was never going to buy it," Simone admitted. "It was so

appalling it was almost surreal! But then you popped up with the perfect garment, and I knew you had an exceptional eye."

Bagot-Black Fine Art specialised in Australian women artists, and Simone, whisker-thin and with an unerring eye herself, had an almost mystical ability to winkle out from attics and basements long-hidden works by bankable artists and persuade their owners to part with them. She had introduced Sheena to her friends as well as her customers, and to a cohort of young creatives, one of whom was the glassblower Seb Parish. Meanwhile, Sheena was learning about the lives and works of women artists from an earlier era, people like Bessie Davidson, Clarice Beckett, and Grace Cossington Smith.

One of her favourites was Stella Bowen, who'd left Australia at twenty and never come back. Stella had known the struggle of making art while propping up a great man – in her case, Ford Madox Ford – and raising a child. Not that Sheena aspired to be an artist, but she was beginning to nurture a secret dream that she might write something about these women and their unconventional lives.

As well as the work on the walls, Simone's gallery produced and sold prints and cards by artists like Dorrit Black and Margaret Olley. Olley had been at the same art school in Sydney as the little-known artist Elizabeth Bunting, whose still life paintings Simone claimed were as fine as many artists who were much better-known.

"It's almost criminal she isn't famous," Simone said. "I think it's because when she came home from Europe, she never reverted to painting the Australian light."

Sheena listened closely. It was these insights gathered from her boss that she loved most about the job.

"Bunting's command of grey is impeccable. In its way, it's genius." Simone, too, relished the talk, the critiquing of art, almost as much as the collecting and selling. "Her work is so elegant, and for a time her luminous northern hemisphere light was quite the rage. But after we won the America's Cup in '83,

Australians grew more confident. We stopped cringing and began to insist on our own local colour." Simone threw up her hands. "And there you have it, the rise of the likes of Ken Done!"

Simone championed Bunting's work with collectors, gratified to be able to provide the elderly artist with a steady trickle of income. It could have been more lucrative for both of them, but to Simone's despair Bunting refused to allow her paintings to be reproduced as prints, or – heaven forbid – as greetings cards. This frustrated Simone, but Sheena secretly respected a woman who would guard her intellectual property so fiercely. She liked to think she'd have felt the same, but the only thing she was protective of was her freedom.

Her uncle's house didn't look much from the street. Inside, the air con roared day and night and the plain brown furniture was worn, though comfortable. Don and his wife Petra had raised two boys and a girl, all of them now settled in the town. With the kids off her hands, Petra went to craft classes, and their walls were crowded with her quilted hangings and framed embroideries.

Sheena crossed the lawn to the glorified shed Freddie planned to move into once the house in Knox Street was sold. The late afternoon light lent it a rustic appeal, temporarily disguising the fact that it was small and bleak and certain to crush the life out of her mother. Inside, Sheena took out a tape measure and noted the width and height of the windows. The acrylic-mix carpet had an odour that no amount of airing would disperse, and Sheena closed her eyes and allowed herself to imagine that it was she who was to live here. Within seconds it became impossible to breathe, and she sank to a squat and sucked in slow deep breaths.

She had left her mobile phone in the city. It was a deliberate choice, made so that Seb couldn't ring and distract her while she decided whether or not she would marry him. After four days, she was no closer to a decision. Sometimes she thought she would have to, because she loved him – his clear grey eyes, his elegant hands, and the wistful expression she often surprised on his face when he didn't know she was looking at him. At other times she thought there was no way. Why did it have to be marriage? Why couldn't Seb be satisfied with them living together? Because Seb Parish was not that kind of man. He wanted the full dream: the woman, the house, the curly-headed kids, the dog. Sheena wouldn't mind owning a dog, but the kids thing could be the breaker. She didn't want children, couldn't locate within herself a single shred of maternal feeling. And whenever she thought about what Seb wanted, her chest felt tight. Wasn't this consumerism, with her the one to be consumed?

The house where Sheena and Jesse had grown up, where Benny had been born and never properly grown, was now almost empty. Sheena and Freddie were camping on inflatable mattresses in the lounge while they cleaned and painted, and apart from the things her mother would take to what she was now calling The Studio, everything had been packed up and sent to the mart. There hadn't been much. When Jesse left on his round-Australia jaunt he'd cleared his bedroom so thoroughly that even at the time Sheena had suspected he had no plans to return. He'd got as far as Streaky Bay, before meeting a girl he didn't want to leave. As far as they knew, he was still there. Her own room had been full of junk, but she had dealt with it easily. Benny had everything he could want in his room at the care home and her mother claimed to be converting to minimalism.

It was almost shaming to see how little of substance they'd accumulated in all those years as a family. There were a few framed photographs from before their father's accident, and looking at them Sheena felt as if the scenes might easily have been staged, that actors could have been cast to take any of their places.

It had been four days since she had drunk a decent cup of coffee. To escape the reproach of Knox Street's empty rooms, Sheena set out on foot to find the nearest espresso machine. Last time she'd been back, The Little Flower Café had still been in business, and its owner Dave Letlow had been wearing his late-wife's clothes. It had taken a couple of years before Dave fully inhabited Dot's wardrobe – graduating from pants, to skirts and dresses – and a year or two more to wrap her scarves around his head to disguise his hair loss.

By now the locals were used to Dave's appearance, and there was a type of plain-faced older woman who so resembled an older man that tourists could never quite be certain. Once Dave saw that no one cared, he had taken to stuffing a couple of socks into Dot's old bras for a better shape to her dresses. If anyone ever tackled him about it, Dave denied he was switching gender. It had been a comfort, he said, straight after losing his wife, to retreat into her things, to feel that he could keep her close. After a while it had become a habit; he was comfortable with it and if that was a problem for anyone else, too bad. Young mothers still gathered in the café after school drop-off for their coffees; girls still worked shifts for Dave as their first jobs. The collectables side of the business had been let go, which was a pity.

Halfway between Knox Street and The Little Flower, Sheena passed the old water tower that had once been part of the town's fire station. Decommissioned when she was still at high school, it had eventually been converted to apartments, and Sheena had tried to persuade her mother that one of them might suit her better than the shed behind Uncle Don's place. The tower reared up out of a brick-paved yard, and seeing it up close Sheena was suddenly relieved that Freddie had rejected her proposition. Its cement-grey exterior had been painted a dull terracotta, but even so, the tower looked a little prison-like.

During the redevelopment, work had stalled and the tower stood empty. It hadn't taken long for school kids to find their way inside. The boldest had chosen a window high up at the back where they were hidden from the street, dragged a ladder from someone's unlocked shed and forced an entry. Later they'd fashioned makeshift steps out of scrounged milk-crates and wooden pallets, and once, a boy called Dougie Marsh who had never been invited to take part, had snuck up in the dark and removed the crates, trapping inside a bunch of boys who were smoking dope. The first of them to make the long jump down had landed awkwardly and fractured an ankle. Later, Dougie Marsh had been hustled into the boys' toilets after school, where he had copped a thorough beating.

Soon enough, boys in hoodies with spray cans had covered the tower's curved concrete walls with graffiti. In a tiny room reached by a spiral of iron steps, where empty beer bottles with the stubs of candles stuck in their necks stood among squashed cigarette butts and fast-food wrappers, someone had spread two old flock-filled mattresses. The room reeked of cement dust, and damp, and piss, but it was private.

The first time Sheena had smoked weed it was on one of those filthy mattresses. That was the year Kat Tate's mother had been diagnosed with breast cancer, and when Kat had more or less dropped out of school, Sheena had started going around with a girl called Riannah, the younger sister of one of the hoodie boys, Brad Angwin. At night the three of them would climb the steps using their phones as torches, and when they got to the top they'd light a couple of candles and Brad would roll them joints.

Riannah Angwin had long blonde hair, and once, when they heard noises below, Brad had joked that if someone moved their milk-crates they could plait his sister's hair and let themselves down by it. He'd been lying with his head in Sheena's lap, the musky scent of his deodorant mingling with the smoke from the joint they'd just finished. Behind black-framed specs Brad's eyes were a brown so pale they were almost golden; Sheena had divined in his blurry gaze how much he wanted to kiss her, but knew that with his sister there, he wouldn't.

Of course, she and Brad had gone back to the tower without Riannah, not even reaching the top of the steps before his hands were on her. In the room, Brad had removed his glasses and put them, folded, inside one of his shoes, which for some reason Sheena had found endearing. Even now, if she closed her eyes, she could conjure a vision of the two of them damply entwined on the lumpy mattress: Brad's warm pale skin and the tiny swallow tattoo on his left shoulder. It could have been sordid, but somehow it wasn't. For a few months she had thought she was in love. Then on one of their secret excursions she'd noticed used syringes lying among the cigarette butts, and when she'd pointed them out to Brad an evasive look in his golden eyes had made her wonder whether he went there on other nights without her, or with people she didn't know.

Halfway through the year, Kat had returned to school. When Sheena had drifted away from Riannah, and from Brad, she told herself it was loyalty to her oldest friend, but some part of her knew that the sight of those syringes had flicked a switch and that even without Kat she would have made excuses not to go to the water tower. Riannah still lived in the town; she was married to a mechanic and they had two small kids. A couple of Christmases ago, Sheena had heard from her brother that Brad had died of an overdose of heroin, and she'd felt a stab of sorrow for those golden eyes, for the little swallow.

No, she wouldn't like to think of her mother living up in the tower apartments, even if it was designer accommodation. Poor Freddie had been carried off by their father in her teens – not locked up, exactly, but definitely marooned – as much by her own limited expectations as by the town's broad, dusty streets. All those sword ferns she'd brought from their gran's old place, filling pots she'd got as seconds from her brother-in-law Jordan Barry, cramming the carport with hanging baskets so that the light in their kitchen was always a greenish gloom. And now, just like that, the old place was empty.

It had happened so easily. Sheena saw again her father's motorbike crumpled at the base of a tree and the flowers people had piled against the splintered wood. She saw herself and Kat leaving town in a burst of bravado, and Jesse loading his third-hand Kombi, the guilt in his eyes and the impatience. All that remained was their mother's devotion to Benny, which Freddie would never escape, and to be fair wouldn't want to.

Sheena walked on, frowning into the open doorway of the betting shop where half a dozen middle-aged men lingered, heads bent, listening, as the drone of a race commentary spilled from a wall-speaker. Years ago her father had been a regular there, and on a Saturday afternoon she would be sent by her mother to drag him home for tea.

Men and their habits: Seb Parish washed his feet, one at a time, in the handbasin in the bathroom every night before they went to bed. The relentlessness of this ritual was maddening, and in the mornings when she stood at that same basin to wash her face and clean her teeth, Sheena felt faintly disgusted. Would he give it up if she asked him to? Possibly. But over time, resentment would tick inside Seb. What did she do that annoyed him? He insisted there was nothing, that he wouldn't change a thing. But that could not be true.

In the front yard of the house next door to The Little Flower Café, two girls were turning a long skipping rope on the concrete path. Another small girl was skipping and another was waiting her turn. Sheena paused on the footpath to watch, tears unexpectedly pricking behind her eyelids as she remembered from her own school days the rhyme the children were chanting.

"Will I marry, tell me so. Is the answer yes or no. Yes, no, maybe so. Yes, no, maybe so."

She raked her fingers through her pink hair. These girls were too young to be mouthing such stuff, too young to understand its importance. She had learned it herself, years ago, and no doubt other rhymes that she had long forgotten, rhymes whose freighted messages had crept into her consciousness before she'd had a chance to raise her barriers.

As Sheena watched, the girl who had been skipping lost concentration. With one tiny mis-step, the rope tangled against her ankles. The girls holding the rope swung their arms, and as the next girl took her place in the middle and the rope began to turn, they resumed the chant.

Sheena pushed on into The Little Flower, where Dave Letlow sat behind the till wearing his dead wife's clothing. Two young waitresses were in the same pale green overalls as she and Kat had once worn, years ago, before she'd known Seb Parish.

# THE TOWER

Dorelia had been conscious when she was helped into the ambulance, but before they reached the hospital she slipped away into the dark. Voices nagged, repeating her name and urging her to respond, but they kept fading in and out. One of her daughters was in the front beside the driver. Occasionally Dorelia heard her anxiously questioning one of the paramedics. She wanted to tell them she was all right, just taking a moment out. The blow to her head had been a shock, but when she thought about it, she could almost laugh. What would Geordie have said! What would Bunty!

She had met Geordie MacCraith on the boat coming home from England. A classically trained pianist, Geordie had been working his passage playing in the ship's orchestra, as well as in a trio that entertained in one of the ship's many cocktail bars. Unusually tall, with elegant hands and an agreeable face, when Geordie had sat hunched at the piano the trouser cuffs of his dinner suit were at least a couple of inches too short. It gave him the appearance of a vulnerable and leggy bird.

Geordie had noticed Dorelia sitting alone with her gin and tonic.

"You had a drooping look," he said, "a little flower someone had forgotten to water."

She had gone to the bar on her own, determined to stick it out and not mind what anyone thought. Sitting alone in public was preferable to being in the cabin, which was crowded with strangers. Only one of her cabin-mates was Australian, a young debutante type from a family with vast acreage in Victoria's high country. The others were emigrating Brits, who constantly plied the two of them with questions.

Instead of sailing home together as they had originally planned, Elizabeth had returned to France to stay with the family she'd boarded with during her exchange. Dorelia had seen her off at Dover, where she was crossing to Calais, while Dorelia was to travel by train to Southampton to embark on the *Arcadia*.

There had been dark circles under Elizabeth's eyes on that last morning, the visible ravages of insomnia. And for Dorelia, who had set out so gaily for France the year before, the return was nothing like she had imagined.

"I'm sorry you have to travel alone," Elizabeth had said.

"I'll be all right. I came on my own, after all."

Elizabeth needed to take a little time, she said, to restore herself to painting. Amos had given her some money, and when it ran out, she would come home. But the course of a life could change in a flash, as Dorelia knew. With the salt wind tugging at their hair, she had hugged Elizabeth and wondered whether she would ever see her again.

On board ship, Dorelia had felt deprived not just of water but of oxygen. Her canvasses had been stowed in the ship's hold, the cost of their transport having soaked up the last of the extra money she'd had to beg from her mother. But already she felt resistant to unpacking them on the other side of the world from where they'd been painted; she dreaded seeing those remnants of a lost happiness that could never be recovered. Dorelia mourned the tall jars of white lilies, the red-checked tablecloths. She had dramatised herself a little bit during that voyage, playing the suffering artist.

Geordie MacCraith had arranged to be seated next to her at dinner. Quite soon she'd started breathing normally again, sucking in the oxygen he generated with his good humour and his optimism. Geordie was returning to take up a teaching position at a prestigious private boys' school in Sydney. Unlike most of the creative people Dorelia had known, he didn't consider teaching a second choice, or believe that it would diminish him as a musician.

They'd made love for the first time in the tiny stuffy cabin Geordie shared with a trombone player, who had been bribed to make himself scarce. By the time the ship entered Sydney Harbour Geordie had asked her to marry him, and Dorelia, smitten for life, had said yes.

It had been Mel who had climbed onto the roof and scaled the tower. She and Gwenyth had called in on a whim, and seeing Dorelia's car parked in the driveway they'd felt certain she was at home. When she hadn't answered the door, Gwenyth had become agitated. She had a key in case of emergencies, but of course she hadn't brought it with her. When they had knocked and knocked, with no response, Gwenyth had leapt to the conclusion that her mother was dead.

Dorelia knew it was a scenario both her daughters were braced for – to enter a room one day and find her staring sightlessly at the wall, her body without life or warmth. Or worst of all, with a taint of decomposition in the air, her having not been discovered for a week. So Mel had volunteered to climb to the tower and look through a window.

At the hospital, Hannah moved bossily around Dorelia's room, straightening things on her bedside cabinet. Her red-rimmed eyes looked like the eyes of some small, wounded animal.

"Is everything all right?" Dorelia said. "You're not ill, are you?"

Hannah shrugged off her concern. "That house you bought is really not safe; it was a ridiculous choice, at your age. When you're discharged you ought to come and stay with us until you're quite well again."

Dorelia protested, but gently. She wouldn't risk upsetting Hannah, who was capable of conniving with the medical people not to let her go.

"You could have fractured your hip, or something!"

"But I didn't. And I wouldn't have been hurt at all if Mel hadn't appeared like that at the window."

It was a mild rebuke, for Dorelia's opinion of a person who would climb onto the roof of someone's porch and peer in at them while they slept was not something she dared share with her daughters. And the common sense of anyone who would smash the beautiful garnet and green stained glass beside her front door was also to be wondered at. In climbing onto the porch, Mel's boot had broken part of the plaster wreath from the little watch-woman. This had upset Dorelia more than the stitches in her temple, her blackened eye, and her ruined blouse. It amounted to vandalism. Mel had improvised a board to cover the broken window, but neither she nor Gwenyth had offered to have the head or the window repaired, they hadn't even apologised for the damage. In fact, the whole episode, as they related it to the medical staff and to each other, was all about them: how *frightened* they were when Dorelia didn't answer the door, how *horrified* when Mel saw her lying in her chair with her mouth open. Then, of course, when she fell, they were *beside themselves*.

Dorelia would see to the repairs, for to leave the little head, especially, would be unbearable. The main thing was to *get* home, for Hannah seemed determined to have her to stay, a prospect that was beyond wearying.

"Max has a new puppy," Hannah said. "It's completely adorable, and it will keep you company while you recover."

# THE HOUSE OF
# FIRST HAPPINESS

One morning, as Mariel McCloud approached her sixtieth birthday, she looked around her house and saw that neither it nor its contents were a comfort to her. The relationship between dwelling place and dweller, between carefully chosen objects and their chooser, was supposed to soothe, to smooth over the relentless, incomprehensible horror that flowed beneath everyday life. But her house and its furnishings were bland; they had no integrity. It was a place without beauty.

Mariel wondered when she had last woken and felt calmed as her eyes came to rest on the fold of a curtain, the fringing on a lamp, or even the fall of light across a smooth plaster wall. She thought of Swan's Hotel, where she'd first understood about the presence of objects. How could she have forgotten a code she had once resolved to live by?

Mariel's house on the fringes of Adelaide's southern parklands was a place, she now realised, she could leave without regret. She and Nick had chosen it for its ease of maintenance, and around the time they'd bought it they had both become slightly obsessed with preparing for their old age. What crept into her mind now was the house on the other side of the world that they had lived in when they were first married. It was in the coastal village of Fairlight in East Sussex, and Mariel was seized with a longing to see it again. She even wondered whether the current owner could be persuaded to sell. Once the idea had lodged in her mind, nothing could shake it.

There was no one to talk her out of such a drastic move, for her family had dwindled and scattered and her friends lived in houses just like hers; they saw nothing wrong with them. But what had terrified her most had been the doctor, who at Mariel's last check-up had suggested that with her asthma, and an inner-ear condition that compromised her balance, she should consider some form of assisted living. Not quite yet, but certainly down the track. Mariel had recoiled – those villages of identical boxes filled with retired strangers – not life, but half-life: she could not imagine herself in such a place, she'd said, not without wishing to die. The doctor, a woman in her thirties, had responded with a pitying look that seemed to say a day would come when she would have no choice.

In Mariel's view, that day was still some way off. There was a lot of life left in her, but no happiness. It was the absence of happiness that decided her: in her old house it might be possible to tap into the residue of her earlier joy, to reclaim something of it, however tenuous. The house, 'Red Roofs', eclipsed all others Mariel had lived in for happy memories. In her mind it nestled against the green rear flank of Battery Hill, between Hastings and Rye. At night she dreamed of its apple and pear trees, its rose bushes, the long herbaceous border and weeping willow. There had been a small patch of woodland with a secret pond, and this, too, Mariel visited in her sleep. The house's proportions were modest. It had been built in the 1940s using red bricks salvaged from a demolished fish market, so it had always been mellow beyond its years. By now, though, it would have acquired its own patina.

Before sleep, she walked through its familiar rooms; in the dark she would still be able to lay her hand upon door knobs and light switches. Mariel longed to lie down again in her old bedroom, the room where she and Nick had fallen asleep holding hands, where they had laughed together in the dark like children. How many times had they made love in that long narrow room on the upper floor? There must have been a finite number, the last occasion on the morning of the day they left.

When they had locked the front door for the last time, Mariel had cried as if her heart were breaking. Life had never again been as uncomplicated. Oh, it had been a long time ago, but having once lived in such a house you carried it with you for ever, and she was certain that when she came to it, the house would remember her.

Selling up was nerve-wracking, but swift. The packing was not too arduous: for years she had been clearing drawers and cupboards to spare someone the grim task of emptying them after her death. All those trips to the Salvo's — she hadn't known that what was to come first was an adventure.

When all was settled, she checked in to the Grand Hotel to rest and gather strength before her long-haul flight. Instead, she found herself wandering the hotel's cavernous public areas like a lonely ghost. The lifts with their smoky mirrors were particularly daunting, for they reflected a woman who looked too breathless and unsteady to be setting out alone on what was probably a hopeless mission. Mariel was reminded of how it had felt to be solitary and adrift in the world when she was young, in that chaotic period before she met Nick. The difference now, aside from her age, was that she did not feel faint at the thought of paying the hotel bill, so that if she *were* to have second thoughts she could stay on a little longer. It was a temporary resting place, of course, a glittering, impersonal world that would retain no traces of her passage. But nothing ventured, nothing gained, as her Aunt Nance used to say. She would cast herself adrift and see what happened.

That first time, she'd been young and strong; she had been beautiful, though she hadn't known it. Now she was a woman with a walking stick and a bag of medicines. Mariel attempted to quell these last-minute jitters by opening the curtains and gazing at the sea. When the wind dropped, she would walk along the esplanade, and once she was on her way, she would be all right.

After the long discomfort of the flight, Mariel decided on a few days in a London hotel to recover. She chose one near Sloane Square, close to where she had once hunted for vintage dresses in the antiques market on the King's Road. London was no less beautiful than she remembered, but more exhausting. Looking down from her hotel window at people peering at their mobile phones, Mariel felt homesick for the twentieth century as much as for her old house. It was unbearable, the way the world moved on and left you feeling stranded.

Nick would never have allowed her to embark on this crazy mission. He hadn't believed in revisiting the past, though she had never understood why. Because Nick's life, both the one he had shared with her, and his earlier life, had been full of things worth revisiting – beautiful houses, enviable possessions, schooldays passed in grand old establishments. An easeful passage he'd had. Still, Nick would have said sternly that their old house wasn't suitable for a woman of her age, that she ought to have stuck with the place he'd left her in, with its undemanding furnishings, its modern wiring and plumbing, its water-wise, low maintenance garden.

The train to Rye left from London's St Pancras station, with a change at Ashford. As a young woman Mariel had travelled this route often and always in a state of high excitement. Her first train journey had taken her to the summer job at Swan's Hotel. Later, after she and Nick were married, she had gone to London on shopping expeditions, or to art exhibitions – always the Royal Academy's summer show. The roll of the train as it gathered speed out of Ashford station reminded her of how the rackety, narrow-gauge track had always given the second leg of this journey a homely feel, and she did have a sense of homecoming, if only in flashes. For between her and the comfort of it was the renewed desolation of never again coming home to Nick, of knowing that their house was lived in by strangers and had been for decades.

Mariel hunted in her handbag for a mint, as a fine mist of rain streaked the window glass. Sheep clustered in the lee of a dry-stone wall. Berries flamed in the hedgerows, and as the train rattled on, the sun flared through clouds, lighting fields dotted with golden hay bales. September's colours. She stared out of the window at the damp blur of the Kentish countryside.

Soon the train was pulling into Rye station, with its signal box that was quaint enough to live in, and its imposing two-storey red brick station building, which Mariel remembered as having been gas-lit into the 1970s. She stepped onto the platform clutching her stick in one hand and a small overnight bag in the other. The figure reflected in the carriage windows was a jauntier version of the woman in the lifts at the Grand Hotel – narrow-shouldered, forward leaning, soft grey felt hat and new black wool coat, both bought two days ago in Selfridges. Under the hat, her hair, silver as a new shilling, was looped below her left ear. At her throat a slender strand of pearls. Mariel smiled grimly at her own reflection: she would show that doubting old girl with the stick that she could manage.

She passed on into the station building, the overnight bag already heavier than she would have wished. As she hesitated near the entrance, a young woman who had been in the same carriage with her from Ashford stopped and asked if she needed help.

"There is usually a taxi out the front," the woman said. "Are you going far?"

"The Mermaid." For the first time on this interminable journey Mariel's lips quivered. "I'm not sure I remember the way."

The woman smiled. "My car is in the station carpark. If you like, I can give you a lift."

Her name was Sally Parsons and she was the proprietor of the Black Cat tea shop in Lion Street.

"Pop in for tea and cake sometime," she said, as she waved goodbye outside the hotel.

The Mermaid was as dark and secretive inside as Mariel had expected. Its soft furnishings were recent, but the panelling, the polished banister rail, the stair treads, were the same ancient, treacle-coloured wood. Hogarth prints on the walls of the dining room were surely the ones she had stared at during lunch or dinner with her in-laws. Her room was snug and prettily furnished, and Mariel fell into the single bed and slept.

On the Hastings bus she took the seat nearest the driver. He would tell her where to get off in case she no longer recognised her stop. In a dream, she stared through the window at houses and cars and people passing. Like a dream, the road unfolded. The Fairlight Post Office was still there at the place where she would step down from the bus. She wondered what had happened to the large postmaster with the lazy eye, who had once sold her stamps and weighed her letters to Australia. He had always contrived to give her stamps with the Queen's profile on them, because, he joked, those were the ones Australians most disliked.

Up Waite's Lane on foot, and her road was on the right. She was looking for the hedge, but the hedge was gone. A new house stood on the site of her apple and pear trees. Someone had divided and sold the land. This was a blow, but to be expected. Next to it stood her house. Without the orchard it looked crushed into its garden. It was bulkier, added to in ways that made it appear squat and swollen. Her heart gave a little bump, and then another: the diamond panes in the sitting room windows were the ones she had gazed through on rainy afternoons. She felt the weight of a book in her lap. The glad leap of flames in the hearth. The impulse to go inside was overwhelming, but she no longer owned a front door key.

A little breathless, Mariel leaned on her stick and studied the upper windows of her old bedroom: surely her shade moved up there behind the curtain. The house was altered, but recognisable. She had come so far to see it – did she want it still? She didn't know.

The following day Mariel returned by the same route, but with a different bus driver. This time she walked the public footpath along the upper boundary of the garden. From here she could see that their old conservatory had been demolished, likely replaced by extra bedrooms and a second bathroom. It was the modern way. The rowan tree in the corner of the courtyard garden had reached maturity. It was laden with clusters of scarlet fruit. There were a few roses still and hydrangea bushes with flower heads the size of dinner plates massed outside the kitchen. The garden shed, shabby in her time, had been made good, its door painted a smart emerald green. Part of the herbaceous border now belonged to the garden of the new house next door. The weeping willow was gone; the wood had shrunk to a few mature oaks and some shrubs. It was impossible to see whether the pond had survived, but Mariel thought not.

She continued along the footpath to Battery Hill and St Andrew's churchyard. Fallen oak leaves littered the grass among ancient headstones. A union jack flapped at the top of the church tower. The lychgate. Parish noticeboard. Inside the church, stained glass windows, dark wooden pews, the chilly calm that fills all old churches.

The Black Cat was almost empty in the late afternoon, and when Sally Parsons appeared in a dark linen dress and white apron, Mariel's mood lifted. It was only the second time she had set eyes on the woman, but even so it was comforting to see a familiar face. These last few days Mariel had rattled around like a lost soul, never even twice having the same bus driver.

"The season is finished now, thank goodness," Sally said. She handed Mariel a menu. "It's a love hate thing we have with the tourists."

Mariel nodded. The town had swarmed with them in her first weeks at Swan's Hotel. She remembered checking-in an American couple, diplomatic plates on their Rolls Royce, and them asking her what time the antique shops opened. Later they had come to reception to complain that the streets were over-crowded, as if there were something Mariel could do about it. The flow of summer visitors had felt relentless, but after the August bank holiday weekend it was like the supply line had been cut.

"I'll have Lady Grey tea," she said, "and a slice of the bakewell tart."

That night in her bed at The Mermaid, Mariel lay awake into the early hours. It was mad to have come all this way and not at least knock on the door. What was the worst that could happen? They could think she was crazy; they could slam the door in her face. No, they wouldn't be so rude. The house wouldn't let them. Because that afternoon, watching the reflections of clouds drift across the sitting room windows, she had felt the house yearning towards her – it was a yielding of the barrier all houses throw up against strangers. She had longed to respond, but a telephone had rung inside and when it was answered she'd not had the courage to interrupt.

The bus driver was the same one as on her first day. Round red face and grey whiskers. Cheerful.

"Visiting your friends again, love?" he said.

Mariel nodded and took a seat towards the back.

Walking up Waite's Lane she felt a little lightheaded. It was probably the jetlag, but it could also be a warning of the vertigo that occasionally felled her. She always carried a pill to take at the first hint of trouble, but usually delayed until the last moment. Now, with the bus disappearing up Battery Hill, and no one she could call on, she took the pillbox from her purse and swallowed the medication.

The day was cool, but Mariel felt clammy. Clammy was not a good sign, but she chose to believe it was anxiety, the prospect of explaining to a stranger why she was knocking at their door. She leaned on her stick, and the swimming sensation receded. On up Waite's Lane – if she'd had a car, she'd have driven further to see whether the Fairlight Stores still operated. In her time it had been run by two men, brothers, she'd thought, but she had been naive then and perhaps after all they had been a couple. They'd worn grey dustcoats over their shirts and ties – relics of the 1940s, even though it had been the late 1970s. The store had an unpolished wooden floor, scarred wooden counters, and the men served each customer with a courtesy she had never since encountered. Groceries on one side and crates of fruit and vegetables on the other. By now those two must be dead and the shop restyled as a convenience store.

As Mariel hesitated beside the gate and looked up at her house, a small blue car pulled into the driveway. A woman got out of it and came towards her.

"Can I help with something?" she said.

Mariel saw a pale, kind face, straight grey hair cut in a blunt bob. Tweed skirt, a soft grey jumper, sensible shoes. And that was all she remembered, until she found herself being helped inside. Up broad, shallow steps. A small ship's bell fixed to the wall beside the front door. She and Nick hadn't taken it when they left because it belonged to the house. The same studded oak door opening inwards. Framed botanical studies in the hall.

"Come in," the woman said, leading the way to the sitting-room. "I'll fetch a glass of water."

Faded pink cabbage roses on the loose-cover of a sofa, crewel-work cushions. Mariel sat down. Sunlight falling through the mullioned windows threw diamonds of warm light across her knees, and the fireplace exuded a smoky odour. The beams on the ceiling creaked, and time folded around her in a swooning curve. Surely if she closed her eyes, she would open them in 1983.

It was then that she noticed the thin grey cat that sat staring at her from the hearth. When Mariel returned its gaze, the cat looked away and began to wash itself, licking the side of one soft grey paw with its narrow tongue and rubbing it over an ear.

The woman returned with a glass of water. "Aldith Ledwidge," she said, her face creased with concern. "Are you feeling all right?"

Mariel took a cautious sip. "I occasionally have dizzy turns."

"I've seen you here several times these last few days."

That shadow at the upstairs window then, it had not been her own shade, but this woman, Aldith.

"Were you looking for someone?" Aldith said.

For one frightful moment Mariel thought she was going to cry. But then she explained calmly that she had once lived in the house and had been taken with a great longing to see it again.

"It was when I was first married," she said.

Aldith sat on a low chair beside the hearth. "I see. Well, I bought the house about seven years ago," she said. "The people before me were here longer."

When Mariel explained that she had travelled from Australia to see it, Aldith appeared momentarily at a loss.

"So far!" she said at last. "I'll make you a cup of tea."

When she left the room, Mariel stared at the hearth where she had so often knelt on autumn afternoons to set a fire and where the grey cat now sat primly with its feet together. The swirling sensation returned. What if she became ill here in front of this kindly woman? She'd been known to vomit when the vertigo was bad.

Aldith returned carrying a tray, and with the gentle rattle of willow-pattern cups, the sight of a blue teapot under a tea cosy,

Mariel's anxiety subsided. When they had both drunk a second cup, Aldith offered to drive her back to Rye.

"I couldn't put you to the trouble …"

"It's just that on Saturdays it can be a long wait for the bus, and you still look rather pale."

So, it was a Saturday, then. Mariel tried to think what day she had left Australia, but the details of the past weeks kept shifting about in her mind.

"Then a lift would be wonderful."

The car was quicker than the bus. She hadn't much time in which to ask the most important question. They were in Rye, almost at the Landgate, before she had plucked up the courage.

"Have you ever thought of selling the house?" she said.

Aldith stopped the car to allow a woman with a pram to cross.

"Why do you ask?"

"Well, I just thought … sometimes people move to something smaller when they …"

"When they get old!" Aldith laughed. "I dare say the time will come," she said. "But not quite yet."

They were outside the hotel, with the car blocking the narrow road. Mariel had to clamber out.

"Thank you for the tea," she said, "and the lift."

The blue car lurched away over the cobbles. Well, that was that, she thought.

On Sunday morning Mariel woke early and wondered why she felt at a loss. Oh, yes, she had seen the house, but there was no prospect of owning it again. Her great adventure had fizzled out and she had been foolish not to have made a backup plan. After breakfast she set off for a short walk around the town. The church bells were ringing when she returned to The Mermaid, and there was a message waiting for her: Aldith Ledwidge would be at The George Hotel at one o'clock. If Mariel was feeling up to it, perhaps she would like to meet for lunch. Aldith had left her telephone number.

Mariel called her at once and accepted. "I feel quite bright," she said. "I've just been for a walk."

"Oh, good!"

The bar in The George was packed, but Aldith had reserved a table in a corner of the dining room.

"My hearing isn't great," she admitted. "I thought this would be quieter."

The weight of a white damask napkin in her lap. A small blue vase with a pink rosebud and a sprig of rosemary. Aldith, sitting across from her wearing a grey silk blouse under a beautifully cut tweed jacket. They both ordered the roast, with trimmings, and a glass of white wine.

Over the meal they swapped stories. Aldith's marriage had ended in divorce; she had two sons, both now living in Canada.

"One went and the other followed." Her smile was resigned, yet the pain of some great sorrow passed across her face.

Dessert. Why not. Apple pie with cinnamon ice cream. They took their time over it.

"You asked if I had thought of selling," Aldith said.

"Oh, I really shouldn't have. It's just that I had this mad idea I could salvage something from the past."

Aldith put down her spoon. "I suppose at some point we've all longed to go back to a happier time." She touched the rosemary in the little vase. "I've never heard of anyone who succeeded, have you?"

"No."

"Will you return to Australia?"

"I don't know." Mariel, too, put down her spoon. "To be honest, there's nothing to take me back. And I'm here now, so perhaps I'll stay for a while."

Aldith smiled then, and in her pale, narrow face the young woman she had once been briefly flickered.

"I was hoping you'd say that, because I've had an idea."

Mariel held her breath. Aldith's eldest son Charlie and his wife Linden had been through a difficult time, with Linden having some kind of breakdown.

"Unfortunately, it's not the first," Aldith said. "It started way back, with her first pregnancy."

The couple had three children, and when each was born Aldith had flown to Canada to help. The grandchildren were grown now, with the youngest about to leave home on an art school scholarship.

"Louis has always been Linden's favourite," Aldith said, "and his going has unsettled her again. I was going to ring one of the house-sitting agencies, but perhaps you would …"

"Oh, yes!"

"There is a cat," Aldith said. "Mavis is twelve, and I think boarding might kill her."

So she would sleep again in her old bedroom. Perhaps the dream of salvaging happiness had not after all been mad.

"It will give you time to decide about the future," Aldith said. "I could be gone three months."

Mariel smiled. However short the future might be, she was already brimming with happiness.

They worked out the details: Mariel would go to Norfolk for a few days to visit her husband's nieces, and when she returned, she would settle in at 'Red Roofs' and Aldith would fly to Canada. They would make enquiries about validating Mariel's Australian driving licence. She would be able to drive the little blue car to the Fairlight Stores.

"It's more of a small supermarket," Aldith told her. "No wooden counters or personal service."

She smiled and offered her long thin hand to Mariel as they parted. "That's all settled, then."

The house had remembered her. At first, Mariel was infused with joy. She slept in her old bedroom, climbing the stairs after evenings spent by the fire with Mavis. But as autumn darkened into winter, she found herself increasingly reluctant to go up to bed. The layout upstairs had been altered with the addition of unfamiliar rooms, and if she were honest, nothing of her and Nick remained in their old bedroom. The nightly patter of rain against the window glass had not changed, but the two of them were not there, and their youthful joy had long been overlaid by something dark and sorrowful. Others had slept in that bedroom since the morning she and Nick had left it for the last time, including Aldith these past seven years. Perhaps it was Aldith who carried the darkness and each night lay down with it.

Mariel moved her few belongings into the room next door, but that had an atmosphere of disuse that was equally disturbing. She knew the discomfort was in her mind rather than in the house, but for all that it was imagined it felt no less real. And in its way, hadn't the house betrayed her all those years ago? Fobbing her off with bliss, when she might have pursued her studies.

After a month, a letter arrived from Canada ... *Linden is going back to work a few days a week. I will stay on while we see how that goes ... if you still ... willing to sell.*

That Sunday, Mariel took the short cut along the footpath to St Andrew's. It was a bleak afternoon, with a sharp wind blowing. Inside, the old church was cold and silent, scented with flowers from the morning's service. Mariel closed her eyes and offered up a prayer for Aldith's son Charlie, his wife Linden, and their children. When Linden was young she had lost her father in a frightful accident. Aldith had written of the legacy of trauma, how she had used to pray that if she could be granted one wish it would be to break the chain so that her grandchildren would not be damaged. *I am not sure that is even possible.*

Mariel's knees protested as she rose from the pew. Before she left for Canada, Aldith had introduced her to the neighbours, Sarah and Len, whose house had been built on what had once been her orchard. They had invited her this afternoon for tea. Sarah's long freckled hands reminded Mariel of her sister Freddie, and as the roof of their house came in sight between the trees, she thought suddenly of the house on the other side of the world where she and her siblings had been raised. A tin and timber dwelling, flimsy in every respect, yet somehow still capable of tugging at her. It had been sold long ago. Strangers lived in it now, as they lived in all her discarded houses, over-writing her memories, making memories of their own.

Mariel shook her head at her own silliness. Her childhood home might be flimsy, it might lack beauty, but she could never deny its hold on her, nor the hold of her native land. Beautiful as 'Red Roofs' was, beautiful as was this sweet green corner of East Sussex, it had never really belonged to her; she had only ever been passing through.

She would write to Aldith and explain that she no longer wished to buy the house, but that she would look after it for as long as was needed. It was a relief to have decided this, and with a steady step Mariel turned onto the path that led to Sarah and Lens' front door. Had she been going to stay, they would have made lovely neighbours.

# THE TOWER

Dorelia had to be firm, even imperious, with the medical staff, though in truth she still felt weak and a little shaky. When Bunty had visited, she'd brought her spare walking stick and left it behind, just in case. Dear discreet and ever-practical Bunty! Dorelia practised walking with it up and down the ward. When the doctor came on his rounds, she was resolute.

"I'm quite all right," she insisted, "and I want to go home."

From the questions he put to her, Dorelia guessed that Hannah had been bleating to him about her forgetfulness and the unsuitability of her living arrangements. There was resistance to her leaving, but in the end Dorelia prevailed. She let them think that Hannah would be waiting for her downstairs with the car, although privately she had resolved to take a taxi. The tower was waiting for her; she would pull herself up into it.

As soon as the discharge paperwork was signed, she dragged on the various pieces of clothing Gwenyth had brought her from home and set off towards the lifts with as much confidence as she could muster. In the hospital entrance, the revolving door gently shooed her onto the street.

What a relief to feel the breeze on her skin, blowing away the hospital smells. In the plate glass windows at the entrance she caught sight of herself – silvery hair askew, for her hair combs had vanished, straw hat jammed on her head at a mad angle; her moth-coloured cardigan billowed around her like a cloak and her face was distorted by swelling, and by the ugly dressing above her eye. She looked like a witch! Dorelia stabbed at the pavement with Bunty's stick.

There was a seat at the bus shelter. It would do while she gathered her wits. Dorelia sank onto it, squeezing her eyes closed against the morning's glare. And then, to quell the rising panic, she reminded herself that all witches were really queens in disguise, and the thought tugged her mouth into a wobbly smile. This was something her daughters had still to learn. And not only her daughters, but all young women. That one day, if they were lucky, the queens would grow old. They would retreat into their towers.

Dorelia remembered Hannah's expression of horror the morning she had spotted her first grey hair in the hall mirror – she had been twenty-three. Her whole body had turned rigid as she stood staring at it, and then, carefully separating it out, holding it like it might begin to multiply, she had found tweezers and resolutely yanked it out. Dorelia had tried to explain that the prospect of ageing was something you carried with you from childhood; life, she'd said, was a rugged training, in which you grew the courage and resilience to bear up, when the world you found yourself living in was so different from the world you had started out in. But Hannah had whirled from the mirror in a fury.

"I'm not going to be one of those women who just give up," she said.

Dorelia thought suddenly of her godmother, May Fleury, and how she'd bequeathed her the means of going to art school. Dearest May had been another thwarted soul, if the stories in the family were true. It was sad the way women had had to make those choices – art or marriage. Probably many still did.

That nurse who had completed the discharge paperwork had reminded her of the midwife Eviane Bell had brought in to tend to Elizabeth in that attic room in Rye. She'd had the same wide white forehead and eyebrows plucked to a fine black line, the same short upper lip revealing a glimpse of rabbity teeth. Oh, that spring morning, with the smell of the river filling the room and Eviane downstairs playing old 78s on a wind-up gramophone to drown out Elizabeth's cries.

The baby had been a girl. Dorelia had thought Elizabeth would weaken once she saw her, but she had not. Amos had arrived by train, bringing with him the Manchester couple who were eager to adopt his and Elizabeth's baby. The man had just gained his commercial pilot's licence, Amos said. Elizabeth had refused to see them, but when they had gone, how she had wept.

Dorelia opened her eyes with a start to see a taxi rounding the corner. She stood up shakily and waved it down with the stick. The driver got out and opened the passenger-side door for her. It was a Thursday morning; she would ask him to take her home via the good bakery and then ring dear Bunty to come and eat doughnuts.

# ACKNOWLEDGEMENTS

During the two years it took to write this book, the world was changed forever. Covid came. My mother died, though not of the virus. I was halfway through writing a story about a boy and a fox and found myself unable to go on. In the early days of the pandemic, many writers and readers became similarly stuck. I learned it had to do with our fight or flight mechanism. But Covid was an invisible threat, and with nowhere to run to that was further than my own bookcase, I sat down and read *Jane Eyre* and afterwards was gradually able to go back to work. Yet the experience of lockdown and the language we were hearing dozens of times a day, words like 'isolation', 'quarantine', and new expressions like 'social distancing', reawakened in me an old fascination with towers. Years earlier I had photographed a medieval round tower at Killala in the west of Ireland, a structure in which, at the first sign of attack, the whole town had been able to shelter.

Once you start thinking about towers, they are everywhere, double-edged, of course, for a place that provides refuge may also confine. A family can be a tower, as can a marriage, childhood, friendship, memory, the past. Home, if one can find it, is always a tower, which is why the inclusion of tower-like features in

Australian colonial architecture, as well as in contemporary suburbia, represents so much more than mere whimsy.

Old age, if we reach it, may be the final tower. By the time my mother entered extreme old age she was the sole survivor of her immediate family and peers. I often sensed her loneliness, though she was adept at hiding it. Although we were always there for her, she had seen and known things that we could never know or see, and at times she seemed to me like a queen alone in a tower. Hers was a structure built of courage, faith, and determination, in which she did things her own way until the end. With her absence I discovered that grief, too, is a tower.

Several of these stories were published in earlier versions. "Life Support" appeared in *Westerly*, "Fish" in a special digital edition of *Overland*, and I am grateful to the editors who worked on them with me. My thanks to Gay Lynch, who read early drafts of some of the stories and gave valuable feedback.

I am grateful to Meg Stewart, and the trustees of Margaret Olley's Estate, for permission to use Margaret Olley's words as an epigraph.

Details of the fictional portrait of Eviane Bell, especially the use of colour, were inspired by *The Black Cap* (1907), a painting by the American artist, Romaine Brooks.

Thanks to my literary agent Fran Moore, who is unstintingly supportive. To all at Spinifex Press, thank you so much for embracing this project, with a special warm hug for Pauline Hopkins. Deb Snibson is owed so much praise for producing yet another beautiful cover.

Finally, love and gratitude to Christopher and Rafael Lefevre.

Other books by Carol Lefevre

## Mumurations

*Adelaide Festival Awards for Literature (Fiction) 2022*
*NSW Premier's Award, Christina Stead Prize for Fiction 2021*

Lives merge and diverge; they soar and plunge, or come to rest in impenetrable silence. Erris Cleary's absence haunts the pages of this exquisite novella, a woman who complicates other lives yet confers unexpected blessings. Fly far, be free, urges Erris. Who can know why she smashes mirrors? Who can say why she does not heed her own advice?

Among the sudden shifts and swings something hidden must be uncovered, something dark and rotten, even evil, which has masqueraded as normality. In the end it will be a writer's task to reclaim Erris, to bear witness, to sound in fiction the one true note that will crack the silence.

… simply perfect and heartbreaking

—Debra Adelaide

Formally inventive and meticulously observed, this is a beautifully crafted jewel of a work.

—State Library of NSW, Judges comments

This is devastatingly good writing

—Christine Kearney, *Canberra Times*

There is something of Elizabeth Strout's Olive Kitteridge in Erris Cleary, as there is of Strout in Lefevre's exquisite calm prose, but there are depths to Erris that are foreign to Olive and that give *Murmurations* some of the suspense and speculation of a thriller.

—Katherine England, *Adelaide Advertiser*

ISBN 9781925950083
ebook available

# The Happiness Glass

*The Happiness Glass*, explores the imaginative terrain between essays and short fiction. The narrative takes us from remote NSW to New Zealand and England through a series of deeply affecting experiences of poverty, domestic violence, loneliness, infertility, adoption and grief. Her writing is sharp, moving, insightful and beautifully poetic.

The literary longings of a studious girl born into a working class family, hot afternoons in a dust-plain Wilcannia schoolhouse; the temptation to stay, and the perils of breaking free – *The Happiness Glass* reflects complex griefs in the life of Lily Brennan.

Lily's story allows the author to navigate some of the difficulties of memoir, and out of its bittersweet blend of real, remembered, and imagined life, the portrait of a writer gradually emerges.

These scenes are worthy of Patrick White. There are many pleasures in this short, cunningly crafted, deeply felt book, not the least of which is consistently good writing.
—Susan Varga, *Australian Book Review*

Lefevre's linking of fact and fantasy is rich, multiplying the experience to induce various resonances and add depth.
—Moya Costello, *TEXT journal*

… a book limned and enriched by feminist thought, probing how women must run rings around literature (and often life) to write themselves into it.
—Cameron Woodhead, *The Age/Sydney Morning Herald*

ISBN 9781925581638
ebook available

*If you would like to know more about
Spinifex Press, write to us for a free catalogue, visit our
website or email us for further information
on how to subscribe to our monthly newsletter.*

Spinifex Press
PO Box 105
Mission Beach QLD 4852
Australia

www.spinifexpress.com.au
women@spinifexpress.com.au